D1166829

Desire & Ice

Also by Christopher Rice

Thrillers
A DENSITY OF SOULS
THE SNOW GARDEN
LIGHT BEFORE DAY
BLIND FALL
THE MOONLIT EARTH

Supernatural Thrillers
THE HEAVENS RISE
THE VINES

Paranormal Romance
THE FLAME: A Desire Exchange Novella
THE SURRENDER GATE: A Desire Exchange Novel
KISS THE FLAME: A Desire Exchange Novella

Contemporary Romance
DANCE OF DESIRE
DESIRE & ICE: A MacKenzie Family Novella

Desire & Ice
By Christopher Rice

A MacKenzie Family Novella

Introduction by Liliana Hart

EVIL EYE
CONCEPTS

Desire & Ice
A MacKenzie Family Novella
Copyright 2016 Christopher Rice
Print ISBN: 978-1-942299-33-2

Published by Evil Eye Concepts, Incorporated

Introduction copyright 2016 Liliana Hart

All rights reserved. No part of this book may be reproduced, scanned, or distributed in any printed or electronic form without permission. Please do not participate in or encourage piracy of copyrighted materials in violation of the author's rights.

This is a work of fiction. Names, places, characters and incidents are the product of the author's imagination and are fictitious. Any resemblance to actual persons, living or dead, events or establishments is solely coincidental.

Acknowledgments

I can't thank Liliana Hart enough for inviting me to into her world and allowing me to play around. And as always, profound gratitude to the wonderful and talented team at Evil Eye - Liz Berry, M.J. Rose, and Kimberly Guidroz, as well as Asha Hossain and Kasi Alexander.

An Introduction to the MacKenzie Family World

Dear Readers,

I'm thrilled to be able to introduce the MacKenzie Family World to you. I asked five of my favorite authors to create their own characters and put them into the world you all know and love. These amazing authors revisited Surrender, Montana, and through their imagination you'll get to meet new characters, while reuniting with some of your favorites.

These stories are hot, hot, hot—exactly what you'd expect from a MacKenzie story—and it was pure pleasure for me to read each and every one of them and see my world through someone else's eyes. They definitely did the series justice, and I hope you discover five new authors to put on your auto-buy list.

Make sure you check out *Troublemaker*, a brand new, full-length MacKenzie novel written by me. And yes, you'll get to see more glimpses of Shane before his book comes out next year.

So grab a glass of wine, pour a bubble bath, and prepare to Surrender.

Love Always,

Liliana Hart

Available now!

Trouble Maker by Liliana Hart
Rush by Robin Covington
Bullet Proof by Avery Flynn
Delta: Rescue by Cristin Harber
Deep Trouble by Kimberly Kincaid
Desire & Ice by Christopher Rice

1

"Danny Patterson," Sheriff MacKenzie growled. "If you follow your hormones into the middle of the worst blizzard to hit this town in years, you're gonna be looking for another job, son, I promise you!"

Danny was willing to bet serious cash his boss wanted to use a different word than hormones, a word not quite suitable for public broadcast. But Cooper MacKenzie managed to keep things clean when he was speaking over the police radio, even when he'd just been forced to grab the mic from the dispatcher because one of his deputies had disobeyed an order.

At twenty-three, Danny was the youngest member of the department, and unlike his fellow deputy, Lane Greyson, he didn't have a second of military experience. That explained why, even though he'd been wearing the badge for over a year, everyone in the department still called him *The Kid*.

Working to overcome that not-so-intimidating title wasn't easy.

It meant always be willing to prove that yes, he really did belong in the department despite his age and lack of experience. That the chance Cooper MacKenzie had taken on him was going to be worth everyone's while. Sometimes it meant being the first to volunteer for grunt work, like rounding up wayward steer during a torrential downpour and corralling them through a gauntlet of aspen, as he'd done just a few weeks before. And it always meant being the first to follow orders. Always. And yet, here he was, going rogue on the eve of one of the worst snowstorms to hit Surrender in decades.

"She's up there by herself, boss," he responded. "When I saw her this afternoon she said she was headed to the old Laughlin Place."

"Yeah, I heard you the first time," Coop said. "Lot of people are going to be on their own during this storm and we gotta be ready to help all of 'em. So explain to me, why is it you're not pulling a u-ey and getting back to the station like I said?"

"Laughlin Place's been empty going on three years now. You really think she's got a working heater up there?"

"What I *think* is Eliza Laughlin grew up in Surrender and she knows how to handle a snow storm. Alone."

"She's been gone a while, sir. She might be out of practice."

And she's Eliza Brightwell again, he thought. *I checked.*

"And she's not your teacher anymore either, is that it?" Coop asked.

"Sir, should we take this to cell phones?"

"Oh, I bet you'd like that, wouldn't you? No. Let's stay right here on radio so I can let everyone with a scanner know that Danny Patterson's disobeying an order from the sheriff because of some schoolboy crush he can't let go of."

He had nobody to blame but himself for this dig.

He'd always had a reputation for flapping his gums. When he'd worked as a ranch hand fresh out of high school, the other men had worried the cattle might all drown themselves just so they wouldn't have to hear any more of his questions about weather patterns and plant life.

It was a mistake, telling Coop about his run-in with Eliza down at Rawley Beamis's wilderness store just that afternoon.

He should have just kept to himself how concerned he'd been to see his former teacher rushing through the aisles as if her life depended on her next purchase. Make that his still radiant, still beautiful former teacher; the same woman he'd fantasized about for years during English class, wondering what she thought about when she got that faraway look on her face while her students were bent over their tests. Wondering if he could grow up to be the man she thought about in those quiet moments.

Surrender was a small town, around 3,000 residents at last count. Maybe if the town, and the high school, had both been just a little bit bigger, Eliza wouldn't have ended up being Danny's English teacher for four years straight, a length of time during which his attraction to her went from innocent crush to full-blown desire. But there was no changing the past, or the size of his hometown, for that matter. And, given his racing pulse when he'd laid eyes on her again for the first time in years, there was no changing his attraction to Eliza Brightwell either.

Still, he should have kept all this to himself and never should have uttered a word of it to Cooper MacKenzie or anyone else in Surrender.

The town was just too small for secrets. A postage stamp of a place, really, nestled snugly at the bottom of a hill, with hundreds of acres of pastureland on either side of one long road. The surrounding mountains were so beautiful they could make atheists into believers, but like all small towns, people here didn't put much stock into minding their own business. It just wasn't possible.

But if Cooper MacKenzie had minded his own business, Danny wouldn't have a badge, a Smith & Wesson, or the patrol car he was currently using to disobey the man's order. He'd probably still be working as a hand out on the Proby Ranch, bored out of his mind and driving all the other men crazy with his constant talk.

True, he'd loved working outdoors, had loved the

changes backbreaking work had made to his once gawky body. But then one night when they were all drinking at Duffey's Bar and Grill, Sheriff MacKenzie had overhead the boys giving Danny a ream of crap about his perpetually running mouth. Big Caleb Watson, their resident Texan, had said the words that finally drew the sheriff over to their table. "Danny, I swear to God, how many times can we identify every type of tree on that spread? If you wanted to be a botanist, you should have gone to the damn college." When he saw the sheriff standing over him suddenly, Danny thought the man might know more about his story than the rest of them did.

Truth was he *had* wanted to go to the local college, but the necessary scholarships had failed to materialize. Coop's brother Riley taught archeology there, and so when the sheriff first offered to buy him a beer, he found himself wondering if the guy might have a line on some night classes or something. But no, the only MacKenzie brother to go into local law enforcement had been working a different agenda that night.

"You love Surrender too much to leave it, but you also love giving people the third degree," Cooper had said. "Sounds like *I'm* the one you should be working for, Patterson."

The next day he'd started saving.

A few days later, he'd signed up for three different online courses in law enforcement.

In another week, he was driving two hours to Myrna Springs to put in hours on their local shooting range, and on the drives back and forth he'd pull over to pick up any boulder pieces he could haul in the back of his truck so he could add them to his backyard gym.

So what if he'd never attended anything close to a police academy or parachuted into Afghanistan under the cover of darkness? By his first day with the Surrender Sheriff's Department, he had the body of a Greek god and the firearms qualifications of a secret service agent.

None of that would matter now if he incurred Coop's wrath, however.

"I just want to check on her, Sheriff. That's all. I just want to make sure she's got everything she needs to stay safe up there."

The answer was silence, studded with some light crackles that suggested interference from the storm's approach.

The ominous, piled-high clouds seemed far behind him. But they only seemed that way.

Contained in his rearview mirror, they looked deceptively small, even though they were swollen with snow and crawling over the peaks like something out of a science-fiction movie.

The cold front driving them was the real monster, however.

It was the middle of April, but that didn't mean it wouldn't be a helluva storm.

Everyone in Surrender knew full well the Arctic was perfectly willing to take their state into its icy clutches pretty much any time of year. Yesterday the temperatures had been in the seventies, but the forecast had been for a fifty-degree drop in less than twenty-four hours. They were already twenty degrees of the way there. The worst part, as always, would be the winds, the powerful arctic winds that could whip an inch of snow into a twenty-foot high drift in no time flat.

When he thought of Eliza Brightwell alone on that old ranch in the middle of that icy nightmare… Well, that just wouldn't do. That just wouldn't do at all.

But Coop was right. She had to know what was coming. Everyone in town did.

All day farmers had been rushing to pen what livestock they could. Rawley Beamis had been prowling the aisles of his store that afternoon, shouting out warnings that he'd be closing down in a few minutes, even as Eliza had searched desperately for a shovel.

Just one really good shovel, she'd told the clerk breathlessly.

But you needed a lot more than one good shovel to make it through a blizzard, and he wasn't exaggerating when he'd said she'd been gone a while. Four years, to be exact.

But her time away wasn't the only thing that worried him. It was how distracted she'd seemed.

Not just distracted, Danny told himself now. *Not just rushed. She was something else. She was* terrified.

Still, the sight of him all grown up, sporting the body he'd worked so hard on, had startled her out of her frenzy. And yes, he'd seen a flare of lust in her expression when they'd first locked eyes. That lust had quickened his already galloping pulse as he'd approached her.

She'd certainly never looked at him that way when he was her student, that was for sure. And yeah, sure, okay, *maybe* his memory of that look was part of what now had him driving farther away from the center of town. Or maybe it was the strange, fragmented conversation that had followed.

"Just checking on some things up at the old place," she'd said when he'd asked what brought her back to town.

"Your husband's place?"

"Ex-husband," she'd quickly corrected him, then clearly regretted it since it made her answer sound even stranger.

"Oh, I'm sorry," he'd said.

"Don't be. I'm not."

"But you're still friends apparently, since you're checking on his place."

"Something like that, yeah," she'd muttered.

Lance Laughlin, the man Eliza had married. Handsome as sin and determined to get out of Surrender as soon as he'd landed Eliza's hand in marriage. His parents had been ranchers, but from a young age Lance had aspired to be everything from a famous actor to a tech mogul to pretty much anyone who just made piles of money and bought yachts. And he'd held these aspirations loudly and in public, and in a way designed to make anyone who didn't leave

Surrender the minute they turned eighteen feel like a sheep's cousin. Worse, Surrender was largely in agreement that Lance didn't seem to have the talent or the work ethic his aspirations required.

Thanks to the miracle of social media, just that afternoon Danny had learned that Lance still lived in a Santa Monica townhouse, drove a Jeep Cherokee, took lots of douchie selfies on the beach and while driving, and when he was just out of the shower and while he was eating and while he was hiking in the mountains. Not a bad life, but certainly not the one he'd bragged about having as a teenager, and his inheritance probably funded most of it.

It was damn near impossible to think of the guy as rightful owner of the Laughlin Place. He'd sold off most of the acres and all of the horses and cattle as soon as his parents died. The home and horse barn had sat empty for so long they now made up the closest things Surrender had to a haunted house. There were even rumors Lance had let the place fall to ruin because he was using it as some kind of tax shelter.

The idea that the woman of his dreams had ended up married to a full-on slime ball, as opposed to just a douche, had always pained Danny more than he cared to admit. He'd wanted her to be happy at least, even if she wasn't going to be his. Even if his feelings for her, still Jägermeister-strong after all these years, were just as Coop said: a schoolboy fantasy.

But now she was divorced. Now she was back.

Back and scared out of her mind. Buying a shovel, and not much else, it had seemed, as a monster blizzard bore down on her hometown.

"You always did ask a lot of questions, didn't you, Danny?" she'd said.

They'd been the last words she'd said to him before she excused herself and hurried from the store. But she hadn't sound irritated. Rather, there'd been a kind of longing in her voice, a longing that suggested a buried desire to tell him more. And maybe, just maybe, a bit of buried desire for him, her former student, all grown up now and carrying a badge and a gun.

When she'd brushed past him, she'd placed a hand gently on his shoulder. Did she just need him to get out of the way? Or had she just wanted to touch him? Either way, he could still feel a tingle right where her hand had come to rest on his shoulder, a tingle he wasn't willing to blame on the cold.

"All right, fine," Cooper finally said. "But I want a quick turnaround. If she's not stocked, get her out of there and bring her down here to the station so we can find a place for her 'till this blows over. What the heck is she doing back after all this time anyway?"

"I have no idea," Danny answered.

"But I'm sure you plan to find out, don't you, Danny?"

"That I do, Sheriff. That I do."

2

As soon as I dig this hole, Eliza Brightwell thought, *I will be done with my ex-husband forever.*

If someone had been able to overhear her thoughts, they might have assumed she was planning to bury her husband's body on his family's old ranch. While the idea certainly appealed to her—had appealed to her several times over the past year, in fact— she was shoveling mud to save her ex-husband's life, not end it.

And possibly to save her own as well.

Or at least permanently extricate herself from the maelstrom of deception and crime that now surrounded Lance Laughlin wherever he went.

He'd been in such a state of breathless panic when he called the day before, she was having trouble remembering any details except the vital ones she'd forced him to repeat. The price this time was $100,000 in twenty-four hours or else the guys —and that's all he'd been willing to call them, *the guys*— he owed money to were going to make big trouble for him.

Worse, these *guys* had been able to find him because he'd been storing some *valuables*, valuables that apparently didn't belong to him, in the same storage unit Eliza had allowed him to keep using after their divorce. The storage unit with her name on it, the one she paid for each month on her VISA. And as a very important sidenote, *the guys* weren't exactly willing to let him out of their sight anytime soon, so Eliza had to hop on a plane, hightail it to his family's ranch in Surrender, and dig up the money he needed. Literally.

The stakes were higher than usual. Much higher. But the whole mess was vintage Lance.

A supposedly well thought out plan gone horribly wrong. A breathless late night phone call where he started explaining the situation a mile a minute, as if she had been in on whatever his latest harebrained scheme was all along and it was her responsibility to catch up. Vague, meaningless terms like *guys*, *valuables* and her least favorite, *big trouble*.

Then, at the end, the stinger, because there was *always* a stinger where Lance was concerned, the telling detail that somehow obligated her to help fix it. In this case it was her storage unit. In the past it had been her credit cards, her health insurance plan and, in the coup de grâce that had finally ended their marriage, her forged signature on some bank documents. But this time she hadn't discovered Lance's little act of forgery before anyone else had. As a result, she'd been implicated in a criminal conspiracy and her name and some of her personal information were in the hands of some very bad guys.

Only now did she have time to wonder why her ex-husband had been burying bags of cash on his parents' old ranch. Before she'd been too busy rushing to make flight arrangements, her heart dropping every time she saw the weather report. Once the ground iced over there wouldn't be a chance in snowy hell she could actually dig up this—

Just call it what it is, she thought. *A ransom. A ransom that will also help some very bad guys forget they ever learned your name.*

She was right at the spot where Lance had told her the cash was buried, ten paces from some wind whipped pines and a tangle of chokeberry nobody had bothered to tame in years.

The hole she'd dug was three feet deep now. Not a peek of the burlap sacks he'd told her to look for.

Downhill, the house was a faint triangle of light. If she hadn't been rushing to beat the elements, she might have taken a moment to enjoy the sweeping view of the valley, a view that stretched all the way to the spot where Surrender's tiny main street was a twinkling blanket of light in the falling dark. But just looking in that direction now meant exposing her entire face to stinging wind.

My fault, my fault, my fault. This accusation rang through her head with each strike of the shovel's blade. *If I'd just taken my name off that storage unit.*

Her girlfriend Cassie's words came back to her, louder than the wind, louder than the shovel. They'd been haunting her ever since she'd boarded the flight to Kalispell at LAX.

The divorce had almost been final then. They'd been sitting at some sidewalk café in Venice when Cassie, a yoga instructor who'd read every self-help book known to man, woman, or animal, had said, "Sweetheart, you're going to be tempted to leave the door open just a crack. Just an inch. Trust me on this one. I did it myself. But with a man like Lance, you need to close that damn door all the way and put *War and Peace* in front of it."

She'd thought Cassie had been referring to how handsome Lance was and she'd resented the implication that she could be so easily seduced by looks alone. In the beginning, Lance had offered more. Affection. Big dreams. An ambition she'd found undeniably attractive. But after four years of marriage she'd come to see all of it for what it truly was. A refusal to be grateful for the blessings that did come his way. A constant desire for bigger, better, flashier. A belief that other people, including her, were always opportunities but never partners.

Now that she'd actually done what Cassie had warned her not to, left the door open a crack, she saw a different meaning in her friend's warning.

Part of her, a part she was ashamed to admit existed, had done it so that one day, they could come back together, not to give marriage another chance but to make their painful past seem like a distant memory. Some kind of fresh start, either as friends or maybe casual, infrequent lovers, that would at least water down the lies and betrayals that defined the four years they'd spent together.

And this was the result.

Another scheme. Another cry for help.

Answering this one might turn her into an ice sculpture in the middle of a Montana field.

Just keep digging, she told herself. *Just keep digging until you can't dig anymore, and then you'll be done. With him. With all of it.*

She stopped when she felt icy pricks stinging the side of her face. In different circumstances, the feel of them might have made her smile. It had been ages since she'd seen snow, much less felt it on her skin. But here, in this field, they marked another hour lost to Lance's latest doomsday countdown.

"Miss Brightwell?"

It all happened so fast she had trouble ordering the events once she found herself sitting on the ground, legs splayed, holding one bloody hand to her chest.

One second, she screamed.

In another second, she saw Danny Patterson standing just a few feet away, blocking out the house behind him.

In another, she lost her grip on the shovel mid-strike and the blade flew up toward her face before she threw her hands out to stop it.

The heat and bite of a serious wound pulsed underneath the glove on her right hand. She went to tear it off. Danny crouched down next to her, stopping her, his own bare fingers gently pulling the glove off her hand, while he whispered, "Hey now. Hey now. Easy, Miss Brightwell."

"You can stop calling me that, you know," she said. "I'm not your teacher anymore. I haven't been anyone's teacher for a very long time."

The deep line in her right palm was filling with blood.

"Yeah," he said, but it sounded like he was studying the wound. "And what would you like me to call you?"

Sucker. Dummy. Divorced. Cliché.

"Eliza's fine."

"All right, Eliza. Well, we need to get you to a first aid kit. I've got one down in my—"

"No," she said, shooting to her feet. "I have to —I just have to get this done before the storm starts."

She closed her injured palm. It made the wound hurt twice as much and sent blood dribbling through both sides of her fist.

"Get what done?" he asked.

And that's when it hit her; Danny Patterson was a *cop* now. Not just a former student. Not just a stunningly handsome and caring former student. He was a cop who had just caught her trying to dig up money on her ex-husband's property.

Whatever expression these thoughts left on her face, it made Danny cock his head to one side.

Snow fell all around them. The house had become a hazy apparition in the near distance. The once expansive view of the valley beyond was now lost to a wintry veil.

A thought occurred to her, fast as a rattlesnake strike and just as venomous.

Danny had always had a crush on her, hadn't he? It had seemed harmless back in the day. At the time she'd been more concerned with the darkness that had threatened to take hold of him after his father walked out on his family.

Could she use some of those old feelings to her

advantage now? Long enough to distract him, at least.

Lord, it wasn't like it would be a chore. He'd certainly grown up to be a looker.

Oh, who was she kidding? He'd find her way too old now, for sure. Four years spent working three jobs to support her husband's bad investments didn't leave a lot of time for the gym. Nothing close to the Southern California minimum of three visits a week.

But maybe the fantasy alone, the prospect of going to bed with one of his old teachers, would be enough to stall the guy for the time being. And it's not like it would be hard for her to act the part.

Not with him. Not now.

Some parts of him looked the same, which was a little creepy. Same bright, inquisitive eyes, the same adorable baby face. But his brown bowl-cut was gone, replaced by a military grade buzz cut that accentuated his powerful neck muscles. And he was taller, much taller, and packing some serious muscle. He stood his ground now with absolute confidence, his leather fur-lined coat flapping in icy winds that didn't seem to faze him in the slightest.

No, it wouldn't be hard. It wouldn't be hard at all. Maybe plant a little kiss on that cheek. Run her fingers gently along that hard jawline as she made a date for later that night. After she had unearthed and hidden the money underfoot. And then maybe—

What the *hell* was she thinking?

Teasing, deceiving, using her body as a weapon and bait? This wasn't her!

This was what Lance Laughlin had turned her into by sending her out here.

"Eliza," Danny said quietly.

"Danny...just. I need you to go so I can work. I'll be fine, really."

"And by work you mean dig, I take it. Not sure you're going to do much more digging with your hand like that," he said.

"I can manage."

"You can manage once we get it bandaged up, maybe."

"Danny, seriously. I need to finish before the storm hits."

"Storm's already here, Miss Bri—Eliza."

"Still, just…"

"Just what?"

"You always did ask too many questions, you know that?"

"Second time you told me that today," he said with an easy smile. "Here's another question. You planning to bury yourself in the ground once you're done? 'Cause there's much easier ways to protect yourself during a blizzard. Like making sure your house is stocked and the heater's working, for starters. So…"

"The heater's working," she said. "I've got two fireplaces going too."

"Provisions?"

"Some."

"Some. Okay. Well, if *some* isn't *enough*, then I've got orders from Sheriff MacKenzie to bring you down to the station so we can—"

"That's just not an option, okay? Now, *please*, just—"

"Eliza, tell me what's really going on before you freeze to death out here!"

Snowflakes laced the freshly dug hole. Fear made the snow hitting her face feel even colder than it was.

In her mind's eye, she saw the hole filled with snow, then ice. Saw herself trying to dig another hole, hoping to hit treasure. And then another, her hands bloody, the shovel threatening to break in the frozen ground.

Fear turned to terror turned to panic and all she could manage to say was, "Danny…" But it came out of her sounding like a plea. When she hit the snowy ground knees first, the first sob ripped from her chest.

"Hey, now," Danny whispered.

He sank down next to her and curved an arm around her back. He hoisted her to her feet. There was something more than warmth radiating from him—something strong and steady and reliable. And then there were his gentle whispers, warmer even than his touch.

"Let's go down to the house, Eliza. Let's get you out of this cold."

3

"I think it's cars," Eliza said once she stopped crying.

Danny had just finished bandaging her hand. Even though he was still a man of many words, he'd known better than to ask her questions while she wept. They were somewhat warmer, but the kitchen had no dishes, an empty fridge, and none of the provisions she'd claimed to have when Danny questioned her.

The walls of the old house creaked like the hull of a ship tossed on an angry sea. The place was empty enough inside to feel haunted, the only furniture the grimy breakfast table where they were sitting and a plastic covered sofa in the living room. Danny had draped his leather coat across the back of his chair. It was the only soft surface in sight and she longed to curl up inside of it.

"Cars?" Danny said.

"It started right as we were getting divorced," she said. "Before that it was some kind of disposable cell phone business. Before that, herbal supplements that supposedly added ten years to your life. But the cars...that's when everything changed."

"And how'd they change?"

"He didn't fight me for much in the divorce. He let me have our condo and our savings. It wasn't much, but he saved me from having to hire a lawyer. Then he bought a townhome he shouldn't have been able to afford."

"So money started coming in right as you were leaving?"

"Yeah, and if I'd wanted some of it, I could have stayed, I guess. The divorce was my idea, not his."

"What about the inheritance? He sure sold off plenty of the land around this place. That probably gave him a bunch of cash."

"Oh, he blew through that in no time and buried the rest of it here on the property apparently. Which I didn't know until yesterday."

"So...cars?"

"Really expensive cars. I overheard these late night phone calls about Lamborghinis, Porsches, Bentleys. And he mentioned the ports. Both of 'em, LA and Long Beach. Last time I checked a new car salesman didn't deal directly with the ports. They work on lots and most of those are in the Valley."

"The San Fernando Valley?"

"That's the one. Anyway, I asked a few questions. But he was evasive so I didn't push. I was on my way out anyway. Right around then there was this big *LA Times* article about this scam the Russian mafia was running through the port. They'd buy temporary visas off people just as they were about to expire. Then they'd use them to lease luxury cars. Then they'd turn right around and put the car on a container ship for Asia where they could sell it for three times what it was worth here. By the time the dealership realizes the car's in the wind, the visa's expired and the visa holder's either left the country or been deported."

"So you think Lance ran afoul of port security?" Danny said.

"No. Port security's not very good, apparently. You can lie on the manifest for a container, just say it's old furniture, and no one looks inside. Also, I don't think port security sends guys to your house asking for one hundred thousand in cash."

"That's some good thinking, Eliza."

"I'm an idiot," she said before she could stop herself. "I'm an *idiot* for letting him use my storage unit. Only things I had in there were some old speakers and a trunk full of videotapes, and he was using it to store stolen cars. I just know it!"

"Do you still love him?"

"That's a complicated question, Danny."

"You know me. I ask a lot of questions."

"No," she said. "Sometimes you fall out of love with people over time, I guess. And sometimes it dies in one moment. Sometimes they kill it. When I found out he'd forged my name on some bank documents, he killed it. That's when I realized the Lance I'd wanted to believe in was a fantasy and I was a fool for believing in it as long as I did."

"Want to know the thing I liked about you most as a teacher?" he asked.

"Sure."

"These words you're using on yourself now. Words like *fool* and *idiot*. You never used them on us, not once. Not even when you lost your patience."

"I think I understand what you're trying to say, Danny, and that's sweet. Really. It is."

"But?"

"But I was an id—"

"Nope. I won't hear it again, Miss Brightwell. I won't let you call yourself those names."

"Fine. Then call me Eliza."

"Eliza," he said.

His bright eyes sparkled when he smiled. Maybe it was a trick of the overhead light. Or maybe it was the flirty, electric energy coursing through him now.

Yes, he still looked somewhat like the boy she'd taught for years, but the intention behind that smile was all grown up, for sure. It was all man, too.

"I used to worry about you, Danny," she said.

"When?"

"When I was your teacher," she said.

Maybe it was her tone that made him flinch. Or maybe it was fine for him to bring up their old relationship, but not her. Either way, it suggested his feelings for her were as complicated as his questions.

"I remember that thing you said to me once," Danny said.

"Lord, which thing? I did have a tendency to go on. Especially when I was talking about *The Old Man and the Sea*."

"You did love that one. That's for sure."

"No shame in being a fan of Hemmingway. He's one of the greats."

"But no, it wasn't about a book. It was about...life."

"Yours or mine?"

"Well, you were giving me advice on mine. But I always hoped you were also talking about yours in some way, even if it was small. I just liked that idea."

"What idea?"

"The idea that you were sharing something with me you didn't share with the other kids."

"Oh..."

"Yeah, there was a better way to phrase that. Sorry. That was..."

"A little creepy, but I get your meaning."

"Do you? Okay. Good."

He blushed when he laughed. And that smile. God, if she could bottle his smile, she'd sip it every morning for the rest of her life.

Now he was hesitant to speak, hesitant to recite the words she'd shared with him that day. That's when she realized it might not just be some old crush after all. A man as talkative as Danny Patterson didn't get a case of clamp mouth over silly old crushes or a reminder of some fantasy from his youth. That was the only thing that could silence a guy like

Danny this quickly—real feelings.

"I remember being very worried when your father left," she said. "Everyone was."

"Well, my father was a crook so it's a good thing he left when he did. Otherwise, we might have had members of the del Fuego cartel stopping by for Christmas."

"Might have made for some interesting gifts," she said.

"You got that right. Merry Christmas, Danny. Here's a kilo of cocaine. Hold on to it for me for a while, okay?"

By the time they were finished laughing, at least three or four out of the three-dozen knots of tensions in her chest seemed to have eased.

"Still," she said. "Learning that someone's not who they say they are. It's rough. I know from experience."

"Right. But I didn't let it take me down, I guess."

But he did look away from her quickly when he said the words, even chewed lightly on his lower lip. Maybe he didn't discuss this part of his life often. Or maybe he never discussed it with women, which meant she was...

She cleared her throat and sat up straight before her crazy, delusional thoughts got the better of her

"No, you didn't. But it did change you. I remember. A bit of the light went out of you. For a little while, at least."

"Maybe so," he said quietly. "But it's back now, isn't it?"

"It sure is," she said, and only once the words left her mouth, once she found herself staring into his eyes as she said them, did she realize she was saying a lot more.

"You kinda brought it back, Eliza."

"What do you mean, Danny?"

She expected him not to answer, to look away again and blush and chew his lower lip a little, none of which would have done anything other than fuel her sudden desire for him. But it didn't matter because he did none of those things. Instead, he stared straight into her eyes with a level intensity that made her sit back an inch and swallow.

"You saw me hanging out on the bleachers one day

during lunch. You said you knew I was avoiding the other kids 'cause they were all flapping their gums about my dad. And then, do you remember what you said? You said I should spend my life trying to find people who judge me for —"

" —what you do," she finished for him, suddenly remembering the moment clear as day. "Not who they think you are or where they think you came from or where they think you're headed, but what you *do*. Who you are in that moment. For them. For everyone."

"That's it," Danny whispered. "That's what you said."

"Well, I'm glad they were meaningful to you, Danny."

"Not just meaningful. Important. *You* were important to me, Miss —Eliza."

"I don't know, Danny. I have to say, my life now probably doesn't measure up to the expectations I set for you when you were younger."

"Yeah, well, we were both younger," he said.

"That's true, I guess."

"I know it's true," he said. "Age is a fact."

"The passage of time is a fact, Danny. Age is more subjective."

"Here's hoping," he said with a devilish grin.

The desire in his expression lit a fire inside of her. She wanted to believe its fuel was stress and anxiety. And of course, the terrible reality that was still waiting for them just a few yards uphill from the house. But this fire, it kept burning. Maybe because she couldn't bring herself to look away from Danny Patterson's intense stare, from the seeming purity of his want, his need.

He'd flinched when she'd first referenced him being her young student. That meant he wasn't just hoping to act out some old fantasy by coming to her aid like this. If anything, he seemed to want to forget the power deferential that had once separated them. And he wanted to forget it because his feelings for her were still there, still real, and now as fully grown as he was.

"I have a confession to make," she said.

"I'm all ears," he answered.

"Out there, when you startled me, I remembered..."

"Remembered what, Eliza?"

"I remembered that you used to have a crush on me and I was going to try to use it to distract you."

"Oh, yeah?" He didn't sound the least bit offended. "How?"

"That's not the point. The point is, it would have been wrong of me."

"I'll be the judge of that."

"Danny. Be good."

"Do I have to?"

"I may not be your teacher anymore, but you're on duty, mister. Unless this uniform and badge are a costume."

That seemed to do the trick. He sat back in his chair and folded his arms over his broad chest. But his smile was lingering, and he cocked one eyebrow as he studied her. And the fact that he took the job seriously enough to respect the uniform only made him more attractive.

"Interesting," he said quietly.

"What's interesting?"

"Interesting that you'd bring that up. Your little plot to flirt me into distraction."

"I wouldn't call it that exactly. But I'm glad you find my confession interesting, I guess."

"What's interesting is you didn't actually do it. Not for one second. And you told me about it anyway. I mean, call me crazy, but why confess to something you didn't actually do?"

Lord, she thought, now *who's the teacher?*

"Unless you want me to know you were thinking about me in that way. Or thinking about *pretending* to think about me in that way so that...you know, you'd have an excuse to think about me in that way."

"Danny. Focus, please."

"On how hard you're blushing?"

"The point, Danny, is that I've told you the truth about everything. But my situation's still the same. I need that money. Now."

"Even if you dig it up in twenty minutes, which you shouldn't with your hand the way it is, you're not getting out of Surrender anytime soon in this storm."

"I could get a picture of it on my phone and send it to them. It might hold them off."

He considered this for a minute. His hands were clasped on the table in front of him, big, veiny hands that were more than capable of digging a hole through icy ground if he wanted. They could do lots of other things, too, those hands. Lots of things.

"You really think these guys are gonna kill Lance?" he asked, jolting her attention back to his face.

"I don't know. I only talked to Lance."

"So these guys might not even exist?" he asked.

"Of course they exist," she snapped. "Why go to all this trouble just to get a bag of cash? He'd just come and get it himself otherwise."

"He could be in some other kind of trouble, just not the kind he said. Not the kind that would convince you to get on a plane for him. Maybe the cops are watching him and he can't leave L.A. The money you're bringing him could be his escape plan."

"Is this your way of saying you're not going to help?"

"Oh, I'll help. But I'm going to help *you*, Eliza. Not Lance."

"Much as I hate to admit it, they're one and the same right now."

"See. That's what I'm not sure of. If we just take a minute to look at the facts, maybe call Coop—"

Eliza shot to her feet. "Cooper MacKenzie? Are you out

of your mind? I can't involve the *sheriff* in this."

"You already involved a deputy?"

"A deputy who barged his way into the situation!"

That got Danny on his feet.

"Well, you weren't exactly inconspicuous, running through Rawley Beamis's store like you were getting ready for the zombie apocalypse."

"Be that as it may, you are *not* calling Cooper MacKenzie!"

"Eliza, what you said to me that day, about finding people who judge you for what you do and not what they think you are. That's Cooper."

"I don't care, Danny. I can't— "

But she never got to finish the sentence because just then the window above the sink exploded.

4

First Danny threw the breakfast table out of his way, then he threw his entire body at Eliza, knocking her to the floor.

When he shoved her toward the gunfire and not away from it, she screamed even louder. But the counters just behind her were the best barrier he could try for, even if the window overhead looked like a bomb had torn through it.

There'd been two separate blasts, both from a shotgun, he was sure of it. Both desperate, wild shots that stank of panic. One had torn through the window above the sink. The second had come in much higher, punching out the top of the window frame and lacerating part of the wall just above.

Kickback had sent the second shot way too high, he was willing to bet. If this guy had aim that bad he was either a full-on amateur, or he was running and firing at the same time. Which suggested he was an amateur.

Maybe his aim was for shit because he'd been coming downhill too fast, counting on the slope to give him a good shot into the kitchen.

That meant he was behind the house. For now.

Danny grabbed Eliza by the wrist and pulled her to her feet. She screamed again but didn't resist. And that was fine. Screaming was fine as long as she could run.

Just as they reached the front porch of the house, the

windshield of his patrol car exploded.

He shoved her back through the front door. Whoever this guy was, he'd rounded the side of the house faster than Danny expected. Now he'd taken up a post behind the storage shed, both getaway cars in his sights. Eliza's rental car, a Buick sedan, was parked a few feet away from his patrol car, further away from the shooter's position and partially shielded, for now.

"Back inside," he hissed.

The foyer walls protected Eliza from any window shots. But no way could they stay here.

A shotgun blast took out the front driver's side tire of his patrol car.

Danny drew his weapon. There was a propane tank sitting in front of the storage shed. He aimed at it.

"You got your keys?" he asked.

"Yes, but your radio. Call for help."

"I can't!"

"What?"

"I can't! I left it in the car so I could sneak up on you!"

"*Danny!*"

"I didn't want Coop bugging me."

"You mean by saving our lives?"

Another shotgun blast took out one of the patrol car's rear tires.

His patrol car was officially out of commission.

But this latest shot gave Danny a better read on the shooter's hiding place; the downslope corner of the shed, which forced the bastard to aim between two piles of stacked firewood that now looked like mini icebergs.

The snow was thick as curtains now. If Danny could just throw another obstruction in the guy's way, the son of a bitch probably wouldn't be able to get a good shot at a moving target. Or two moving targets.

"Phone?" he asked.

"Turned off years ago."

"Where's your cell?" he asked.

"Kitchen. Where's yours?"

"Kitchen. In my jacket."

"Well, goddammit, should I go and get—"

"No! Stay right here!"

Best-case scenario was they were dealing with one lone fucker. Worst case was reinforcements were on their way and the house would soon be surrounded. There was no splitting up. Not as long as the house had windows. And now the kitchen had one destroyed window and a gaping hole in the wall.

They had to get out. Now. The patrol car and the radio inside of it were no longer options. That left her rental car.

And that grimy old propane tank in front of the shed.

"Give me the keys," he said.

As soon as he reached back, she pressed the Buick's keys into his palm with a shaking hand.

"I'm going to fire three shots at that propane tank," he said. "After the third one, we run for the Buick."

"The propane tank's been empty for years."

"I don't need it to blow up."

"Well, it won't blow up. Haven't you seen *Myth Busters*?"

"*Stop talking about* Myth Busters *when I'm trying to save your life!*"

"*You know what would have saved our lives? Your radio!*"

"Third shot! Run after the third shot! Got it?"

"Yes."

He turned and fired the first one before she could argue.

Taking aim through the billowing, swirling snow wasn't easy. But he managed to hit one of the propane tank's struts; he could hear the metallic ding over the howling wind.

He wasn't lying. He didn't need it to blow up. He just needed it to move.

The second shot hit the strut. Maybe, just maybe, the

asshole behind the shed didn't know you'd need full-on explosives to make a propane tank blow, because he wasn't firing back. He might have gone into retreat. But that was best case. Too best case.

"Get ready," Danny said.

The third shot knocked one end of the propane tanks sideways off its stanchion. Not far enough. But a good start.

They ran for the Buick. Danny kept firing.

It felt like the only parts of his body that still worked were his feet, his eyes, and his trigger hand; the rest of him felt numb. His shots played music on the propane tank's hull and then finally the tank flew off its stanchion and went rolling into the woodpiles just as he'd hoped, toppling one pile of cut wood onto the other, cutting off the shooter's line of sight.

Eliza plastered herself to the floor of the backseat, gasping. He got behind the wheel.

No radio. No cell phone. Just a fucking Buick.

The car started. No response from behind the shed.

Through blinding snow, tires skidding, he spun onto the access road that led to the highway. And that's when he realized this wasn't going to be a quick getaway.

A set of headlights came bouncing around the opposite side of the house and started downhill.

"Where is he?" Eliza cried.

"Stay down!"

The fear the propane tank might blow hadn't forced the guy into the retreat. Instead, he'd cut bait and gone for his wheels.

"Son of a bitch," he cursed.

The black Explorer crossed the house's front drive behind them and sped down the hill off to their right, trying to beat them to the highway. Trying to block the path back to Surrender.

"This fuck might have shitty aim but he sure is persistent."

"Who is he?" she cried.

"Escape first, ask questions later."

The guy drove with confidence. Was he a local? Or maybe he was just crazy taking to the snowy grass like that. Either way, the Explorer made it to the highway before Danny did.

"Well, if he's driving then he can't—"

Muzzle flare bloomed next to the Explorer's passenger side window. A second gunman, a second gun. The Buick's windshield pocked. Not a shotgun blast this time, but the same shitty aim. Same psycho persistence.

He turned just in time, put the gas pedal to the floor.

"Where are you going?" Eliza screamed.

"You'll see."

"I don't want to see. I want you to tell me where we're going."

No way in hell was he going to do that. He had a plan, but it was a crazy one, the kind you just went ahead and did and then asked forgiveness for later if it went to hell. If you were still alive by then.

A few minutes up the road was the land where he'd helped some ranchers corral their wayward steer during the big rainstorm a few weeks before. After they'd roped the soaked cows, it had taken hours to guide them through the trees, hours in which, he hoped, he *prayed*, a map of those woods had engraved itself on his memory. Because now he was going to have to drive it in the blinding snow. And he was going to travel it in the opposite direction of the one he and some pissed-off cows had walked that night.

"You are driving in the opposite direction of Surrender!"

He was about to say something to quiet her, but just then the rear window blew out in a shower of tempered glass.

All things considered, he shouldn't have been that excited to see a roadside cross. But it marked the spot where they'd reached the highway with the cows that night. So he turned toward it, praying for forgiveness as it disappeared beneath his tires.

Eliza screamed as the Buick plowed straight toward a thicket of trees, bouncing over rutted and uneven earth, snow pelting the windshield like falling rocks.

But so far, he was remembering the curves and the breaks, same as he'd walked them that night, boots sinking into the mud, a symphony of pissed-off moo's filling the wet woods behind him. Only now it was Eliza's terrified screams behind him. They were a lot louder.

A tree took off the driver's side mirror.

Eliza went silent. He figured she'd pressed her face to the floor of the backseat so she wouldn't have to see the chaos just outside the Buick's windows.

At least there was no more gunfire. The bastards were following them for sure. But trying to navigate the thick woods had taken the confidence out of them.

Danny knew there was a sharp uphill climb just ahead. The bastards on his tail didn't. He gave the Buick the gas he knew it needed to mount the sudden slope. Then he turned to the left about forty-five degrees, aiming for the next break in the trees. It was a two-fold maneuver he accomplished in the nick of time.

Unfamiliar with the landscape, his pursuers would fumble one of those moves. He was counting on it.

The passenger side of the car dragged along an aspen trunk with a sound like God's fingernails on a chalkboard. Still, he'd given the Buick enough power to start the climb and they were speeding uphill now.

Just as he'd hoped, the SUV wasn't so lucky.

Through swirling snow, he saw their headlights lurch as they hit the slope without enough speed.

He wanted to gloat, but he had to keep his focus on the woods in front of him.

The path uphill was snaky at best.

After another few minutes, there was still no sign of the Explorer.

The snow was too thick now to see all the way to the base of the hill.

But by God, it looked like they'd really lost them. Maybe the Explorer's 4-wheel drive had crapped out or maybe it didn't have it to begin with. Or maybe one of the sharp uphill bends had taken them out, but it didn't matter, because they needed to keep—

The Buick's nose slammed into an aspen trunk.

The car came to a dead stop and Eliza hit the back of the driver's seat.

When he looked up, he saw branches and icy leaves filling the windshield.

"You okay?" he shouted.

"Define *okay*."

"Can you run?"

"Yeah, I can run. Are they still coming?"

"I don't see 'em. But we still need to run."

He could only open the driver's side door a foot or two. He'd been so busy savoring his temporary victory he'd driven them straight into a prison of branches.

Eliza fought her way out of the backseat and into his arms. Then he was clawing their way out. Her bandaged hand kept her from helping, so she held on to the back of his pants with her good hand and rested the other one against his shoulder.

"So much for running," she said.

"The Flynns have a hunting cabin up ahead."

"How do you know? How can you even tell where we are?"

"Some ranchers lost some steers out here in a big rainstorm a few weeks ago. They were all up and down this hill and we had to rope 'em and bring them to the highway one at a time. We used one of the Flynns' cabins as a base of operations."

"Does it have a phone?"

"No, but it's got some wood and a wood stove we can

use to keep warm until this blows over."

"And what about them?" she asked.

The brush cleared up suddenly, which meant he could stop grabbing at icy branches with his bare hands.

She looked behind them. Just a dark slope filled with thick veils of snow.

No headlights, no gunfire. No sound of anyone clawing through the woods after them. Although with the way the wind was howling now, they wouldn't have heard the approach of anything smaller than a C-130.

When her eyes met his, there was pure, unguarded fear in them. Despite the bitter cold, despite his stinging hands, he could only feel one thing—his desire to take her fear away. Right then, right there. For all time.

"Danny, what happens if they find us out here?"

He took her face in both hands and spoke before he could measure his words.

"Then I'm going to have to kill those sons of bitches."

He wasn't sure if it was the life going out of her or the fight. The latter wouldn't be so bad. Acceptance, in this type of situation, was a good thing. Acceptance didn't always mean rolling onto your back and letting life roll over you like an eighteen-wheeler. It meant admitting you'd been pushed to that dangerous place where the only choice left was to draw your weapon.

And he certainly didn't mind having her in his arms. It helped him to breathe. And breathing was important, even when you were running for your life, even when you were haloed by snow that stung your neck, face, and hands.

"Let's go," she finally said, with a newfound authority in her voice.

5

"Wait!" Eliza cried.

Danny had just pulled some firewood off the stack in one corner of the hunting cabin.

"A fire? Really? They'll see the smoke."

"Not in these winds," he answered. "And we'll freeze to death without it."

"Are you sure?"

"On both counts," he said. "Trust me."

Oh, how she wanted to. But as soon as they'd reached the cabin, her only recurring thought was, *We're going to die here.* Starved, shot, or frozen to death. One of those would do the trick, for sure.

She shivered fiercely.

If Danny couldn't get a fire started, they'd probably have to wear her coat in shifts.

Back at the ranch she'd been crying so hard when they first stepped inside, she'd neglected to take the thing off. That was the only reason she'd still been wearing it when the gunfire started. No such luck for Danny. His fur-lined jacket was still there, probably lying in a ball on the kitchen floor where it was laced with paint dust and other debris.

"Time to worry about the fire will be when the storm dies down and the wind stops dispersing the smoke," he said.

Her pulse slowed when he found a box of matches

under the wood stove.

"By then, we'll be out of here, I promise. Coop's already looking for us, I'm sure."

"How's that?" she asked, rubbing the sides of her crossed arms.

"He wasn't pleased when I told him I was headed to your place. He said make it quick. When it's not quick and I don't answer his radio call, he'll strike out looking for me if only to beat my ass into the snow."

"Not even Cooper MacKenzie could get far in this storm. Neither will a search party."

"Yeah, and neither will the assholes who tried to kill us."

"I hope so."

The cabin was just a single room with a stack of firewood and a wood stove against one wall. A sheet of plywood slid easily into place inside over the single window, the first thing Danny had tended to once they stepped inside out of the blowing snow.

The door had been secured by a padlock when they arrived, but Danny knew the code from when he'd used this cabin for his rain-drenched cattle roundup, which, to be perfectly frank, sounded like a beach vacation compared to what they were going through now. Now the padlock was on the inside latch, and the sight of it comforted her each time she imagined bullets punching through the walls.

If the storm had been giving the Laughlin Place hell, it was giving this little cabin hell and then some. But each time the walls shook from the howling wind, Eliza felt an ironic burst of comfort, because it meant the storm was either threatening the lives of the men who'd tried to kill them or driving them farther away.

Preferably, both.

But still, fear kept coming in waves that made her pace and rub her hands together.

"God, I could just strangle you for leaving your radio in the car," she said before she could stop herself.

"If that's your thing, go right ahead."

He was using some half-burned newspaper in the stove for kindling, but it wasn't enough.

"Don't be flip," she said.

"Honestly, if it'll make you feel better, I'll let you put your hands around my throat and we can play act, or role-play, or whatever you Californians call it."

"You could have just left it clipped to your belt and turned it off. "

"I could have." The first straining flames fought backdrafts through the chimney pipe. Danny reached into his pocket, pulled out a switchblade, and used it shave slender splinters from one of the pieces of wood stacked in the corner.

"But it wasn't just about the noise, was it?" she asked.

Why was she beating him up like this? Because she was frightened and freezing and terrified they'd never get out of this cabin alive.

"It was about appearances too, wasn't it? No radio on your belt means it's just a casual visit, right? An old student dropping in on his teacher, right? When really you knew I was up to something and you were trying to catch me and—"

Danny shot to his feet. Behind him, fire bloomed inside the stove, filling the cabin with flickering orange light.

"I didn't think you were *up* to something," he said. "I thought you were in trouble and I wanted to help. And yeah, maybe part of the reason I drove out to your place is because when I saw you at Rawley's my heart damn near stopped and I felt like I was fifteen years old again and staring up at the smartest and most beautiful woman I'd ever met. And you want to know why I felt that way? 'Cause it's eight years later and you're still the smartest and most beautiful woman I've ever met.

"So yeah, I took the radio off because I didn't want you to see Danny the cop. I wanted you to see Danny the man. Danny who wasn't a boy anymore. Honestly, if I'd had my druthers, I would have gone home and changed into civilian clothes, but I didn't have time with this damn storm. And I could tell you were scared out of your mind so I didn't want to waste any. Okay?"

"Oh, Danny," she managed.

"Look, I know you're still scared, and I know this isn't over yet. But don't put bad motives in my head 'cause you think it'll make me easier to control. I'm not easy to control, Eliza. Not when it comes to you. Just ask Cooper MacKenzie."

"I'm sorry. You saved my life and I was talking to you like you...Like you..."

Amazing that he took her in his arms after the way she'd just spoken to him. Lance would turn tail and run from any sign of her anger and fear. But Danny guided her to one wall, and within seconds, they were sitting on the floor together, his arm curved around her back, sharing in each other's warmth.

"How many bullets do you have left?" she finally asked.

"Enough to take down two tourists who've got too much confidence and shitty aim," he said.

Sitting forward slightly, he pulled his gun from the holster and set it sideways on the floor next to his feet, handle pointed toward him.

"So you think it's just two guys?" she asked.

"Saw 'em in the car. One was driving, passenger had a handgun."

"Who are they?" she asked. "You think they're the same guys who have Lance?"

"Or they work with 'em."

"But why start shooting at us like that?"

"My guess is they found the hole and figured you'd made off with the money."

"Which meant they knew the money was there in the first place."

"Yeah, that part's harder to figure," he said, and his voice made it sound like he was trying to figure it out even as they spoke.

"Not if they killed Lance it isn't," she countered.

"Don't go there yet."

"Okay. But still... If they thought I was trying to steal the money, why not sneak up on us and take the bag from us at gunpoint? Why start firing like they're trying to mow down a bunch of walkers?"

"I don't know, but everything about it says fear. Not just fear. Panic."

"And dumb," she said quietly.

"That too."

She smiled even though he couldn't see it, what with her face pressed to his chest.

"I'm sorry," she whispered.

"For what?"

"For getting you involved in this."

"Got myself involved."

"Still..."

"That's right. Just be still. Try to relax."

"Now who's the teacher?" she said quietly.

She felt his fingers twine gently through her hair. He stroked her head tentatively at first, and then, once she snuggled more into his body, tenderly.

"Danny?"

"Yes."

"That part about me not being an idiot. Say it again, if you don't mind."

"I'll say it as many times as you like. You're an amazing woman, always have been. You just take too much responsibility for other people's weaknesses, that's all."

"I guess that's true," she said. "But I've never been quite sure how to love people otherwise."

"Well, you've got plenty of time to learn. Everyone does until they're, you know..."

"Dead?" she asked him.

"I was trying to find a different way to put it given the circumstances but... Too late, I guess."

"I appreciate the effort."

"We're not going anywhere, anytime soon. Less it's to the sheriff's station once this storm blows over. Promise."

"Thank you for promising. Even if it's not true."

"It is true," he said. "I always keep my promises."

"How many shootouts have you fought your way out of?"

"I'm doing pretty good tonight, aren't I?"

"You are. I just... I don't want you to feel like you have to save me."

"But see, I do, Eliza. I do have to save you. Part of me feels like I was born to."

She took his hand in hers, holding it gently against her chest.

For a while they lay there in silence, listening to the storm's fury. With each minute that passed without a gunshot or any other signs of human life outside, her heart rate slowed, and her fear felt more like an idea than an affliction.

Soon, the idea that they were still in mortal danger was competing for headspace with the feel of Danny's fingers as he gently stroked her forehead, the warmth of him beneath her and the fire's welcoming glow.

She remembered blizzards like this when she was a girl. Massive, world-ending things that brought life outside to a complete halt. If those killers were still struggling through the woods, frostbite would already be going to work on them, she was sure of it.

Of course, there was the terrible possibility they'd managed to drive up the rest of the slope and follow their footprints to the cabin. But if that was the case, they would be shooting up the door by now, and the idea of them staking out the house in this weather was absurd; they'd barely be able to stand upright in these winds, much less survive the night.

Between his body heat and the spreading warmth from the stove, her own jacket had become unnecessary.

When she sat up, he gave her a startled look. There was fear in his expression, not a fear of being murdered in this cabin, a fear of losing her touch for good. Then, as she slid her arms free from her jacket, one after the other, his eyes glazed over, as if this casual disrobing were as charged and intimate as stripping down to her underwear.

No man had ever looked at her quite this way. She wanted to call the look protective and vulnerable, but that wasn't quite it. If she was reading him right, what frightened him was the idea that she might not let him protect her.

It had been a very long time since a man had worked this hard to keep her safe. For four years, she'd been the breadwinner, the rock, the voice of reason. And before that, the teacher, the surrogate parent, the counselor. Now she was…she didn't know what exactly, but she liked the way it felt. A lot.

"You going somewhere?" he finally asked her.

"No," she answered.

"Good. 'Cause that wouldn't be safe."

Just then, his hand found the side of her face, a gentle, hesitant touch. A touch that reached across years of memories and old versions of themselves.

"That wouldn't be safe at all," he whispered.

She could feel his fingers right at the edge of her lips. Before she could think twice, she turned her head just enough to give them a kiss. He closed his eyes. The air between them seemed to vibrate. Her heart raced from a new emotion that made the fear of the past few hours seem like a distant memory: desire.

"Do you have any idea the things I'd do to you if I didn't have to watch that door?" he said.

She responded by taking one of his fingertips gently between her teeth, then she gave it a light squeeze.

"I believe when I was your teacher I always encouraged you to give specific, concrete examples," she whispered.

"Oh, I can't even get started. 'Cause if I do, the only thing that'll exist for me in the world is what I want to do to your body. And right now, I gotta keep you safe."

"I understand," she whispered. "I guess there's a perfect time for everything."

"There's never a perfect time for anything. Some times are just better than others to try for perfection. And with you, Eliza, that's exactly what I'd try for. Perfection."

Control yourself, Eliza. He's right. This isn't the time.

"You always were such a nice boy," she said.

So much for controlling myself, she thought. *I sound like a porn star.*

"And once I have you all to myself I'm gonna show just how nice a boy I can be."

Just one kiss.

That was all.

She'd just give him one little kiss. Something to warm them, distract them and tide them over until they could be alone with all these explosive new feelings.

The next thing she knew she was on her back, their mouths locked, tongues finding their mutual rhythm. The thoughts flying through her head told her this was stupid, wrong. So what if he wasn't her student anymore, hadn't been for years.

They were still trapped. They should be watching the door, the window. They should be doing anything other than discovering they kissed like they were born to kiss each other. He broke suddenly, gazing into her eyes, shaking his head slowly as if he were as dazed by this sudden burst of passion as she was.

"I think..." he tried, but lost his words.

"What do you think, Danny?"

"I think if we just keep our eyes on the door, we'll be fine."

"Okay."

Was he putting the brakes on? She wasn't sure. It was the most sensible thing to do, that was for sure. He slid off her and sat up, back against the wall, eyes on the door. She did the same. But he curved an arm around her back and brought her body sideways against his. It was awkward at first, but then he positioned her so that she was lying halfway across his lap.

"Now that I'm watching the door," he said, unbuttoning the top few buttons of her blouse, "I think we'll be fine."

"Oh, yeah?"

He brought his fingers to his mouth, moistened them with his tongue, then dipped them between the folds of her shirt. Slowly, he wedged them under the cup of her bra. When he found her nipple underneath, he said, "Yeah. Just fine."

In an instant, her body was flush with goose bumps.

Eyes on the door, his gun within easy reach, he circled her nipple with his moistened fingers. His precision and restraint combined to make her wet in other places as well. She'd seen the passion in his eyes, a youthful crush that had matured into a man's desire. But now, he was willing to delay his own gratification so that he could protect her and pleasure her at the same time.

"Let me give you a little help there," she whispered.

Without getting up, she reached back and unfastened her bra.

It fell away from her breasts slightly, still trapped within the confines of her blouse, which she wasn't about to remove.

She was facing the door too. It only seemed fair.

And she didn't want to distract Danny again by rolling over onto her back and offering herself up to him. Then he might lose all control. As much as she wanted him to, now wasn't the time. Now was the time for this sweet, prolonged torture, for the slow and leisurely way he was testing her nipples with his fingertips. Searching for just the perfect spot. The perfect amount of pressure that would make her muscles tense and her breaths sharpen into gasps. For some reason, dividing his focus between the door and her body seemed to make him highly responsive to each sound of pleasure coming from her.

"See, we'll be fine as long as I keep my eyes on the door," he said.

"More than fine," she whispered.

The wind howled. His fingers traced her breasts. Her folds moistened.

"So that thing you said." He unbuttoned her jeans. "About concrete examples."

"Yes," she said between gasps.

He parted the flaps of her jeans enough so he could slide three fingers under the waistband of her panties.

"When the moment's right, when I've got you all to myself, safe and warm and home, what I'm doing with my fingers right now..." He traced her folds with two fingers, dragging them gently toward her aching bud. "I'm going to do this with my tongue. After I kiss every inch of you, of course. After I use my mouth to show you what a man I've grown up to be."

"Danny..."

"Yes, Eliza."

Not Miss Brightwell. Not anymore. She was Eliza and he was Danny, both adults now, brought together by circumstances beyond their control. Now his heat and desire sustained her, wrapped her in comfort and pleasure on one of the darkest, most terrifying nights she'd ever known. And that was part of the pleasure, she had to admit. The defiance of it. The refusal to be terrified into submission by anonymous gunmen in the icy dark. As if Danny was thumbing his nose at their pursuers by leisurely, attentively fingering her clit. Worshiping it gently and easily and without the crazed, porn-star acrobatics that had always defined her ex-husband's ineffective work in that area.

Each subtle, precise move of Danny's fingers convinced her he had all the time in the world to devote to pleasing her. The truth of their situation was more troublesome, for sure, but not right now. Right now there was only his desire to protect, his hunger to please.

For the first time in hours, she didn't feel a suffocating pressure to rush, to dig, to solve. Didn't feel a need to do anything other than luxuriate in the pleasure Danny was managing to give her with one skilled hand, one hand and all of his senses, which he'd tuned to the frequency of each wave of pleasure coursing through her body.

With his other hand, he reached down and gently brushed her bangs back from her forehead. Something about the combination of this tender gesture and the hungry ministrations of his fingers sent her to the edge. She bit back the scream that wanted to erupt from her, a scream of surprise as much as bliss.

When was the last time an orgasm had gripped her this suddenly and totally? She couldn't remember. Which was a good sign the answer might be *never*. Was it the stress of the situation? The sense of doing something reckless and forbidden? It didn't matter. It was powerful enough to obliterate her thoughts as she gasped into lips Danny suddenly brought to her own.

It was the first time he'd dared to look away from the door since they'd started this hot little session. When she opened her eyes and stared up into his, an aftershock of pleasure rippled through her.

"Where'd you learn how to do that?" she whispered.

"From you." His answer baffled her. "Seriously. No magic to it. Just take a woman who's given all of herself to other people for as long as she can remember, and tend to her needs with no thoughts of your own."

"Given the way most men are, that sounds like magic."

"If you say so, Eliza."

"I do. I do say so."

He kissed her again, gently. Then he sat up straight and returned his gaze to the door as he gently stroked her bangs back from her forehead, reminding her of the combination move that had filled her with pure bliss. Danny Patterson was defined by delicious contradictions. He gave pleasure while offering protection. He could flirt while speaking with the voice of reason.

Her girlfriends, and her mother, and her grandmother, for that matter, always preached the gospel that a man could only be one thing. Bad boys were always bad, even if they could rock your world between the sheets. That was fifty percent of what made them bad, of course. The good fifty percent. But still. A bad boy was a bad boy and you didn't marry bad boys because whenever they weren't going down on you, you usually wanted to pitch them headfirst into a jet engine.

Good boys, on the other hand, were better at listening and keeping their promises than making your toes curl. But as long as there were showerheads and romance novels, you could make do. And you'd always have a nice, loyal companion once you dried off.

God, how she'd always loathed this logic. Had hated how it controlled most of the women in her family, in her life, forcing them into rushed, jerry-rigged relationships with guys who weren't even close to being the one. But she'd never met a man whose very being disproved any of it.

Until now.

Danny Patterson was good and bad at the same time: a savior with a sweet mouth and dirty fingers. Fingers he was now gently licking clean of her essence after working her over in a way that made her feel delightfully violated. Now he politely, gently buttoned her jeans and smoothed them into place. He curved an arm around her and snuggled her closer into his body so he could keep watching the door while he savored their combined warmth.

"So...do I get an A?" he asked.

"Okay. You have to quit that now."

"Aw, come on," he whined. "We can have a little fun with it, can't we?"

"I don't know. We'll see. Maybe once we're out of this cabin."

"After all, you're the one who just called me a nice boy."

"I remember."

"So...I'll repeat the question."

"A plus, you sexy bastard. With a gold star and a bunch of extra credit."

"Excellent."

"Can we be done with that now?" she asked.

It was kind of hilarious they were having this intimate exchange with the two of them back in their previous positions, her head resting on his lap as he sat cross-legged with his back against the wall, both of them staring at the padlocked door. She'd make a note to laugh about it later, once they were truly safe.

"For a little while. Sure."

"Danny..."

"Yes, Eliza."

"We're gonna get out of this cabin, right?"

"What's the rush? I can think of plenty of other things I can do to your body without taking my eyes off the door."

"Be serious, Danny."

"We're gonna be fine, Eliza. I promise. Soon as this storm lets up, Coop's gonna be on our trail if he isn't already. First place he'll go is the ranch and first thing he'll see will be my patrol car all shot to hell."

"Yeah, but how will he find us here?"

"We're not that far away, for one. And second, a bunch of us worked the cattle roundup that night so it's fresh in everyone's minds. We were all right here in this cabin getting our supplies together just a few weeks ago. He'll find us, I promise."

"Wow."

"What?"

"You really were thinking this all the way through, the whole time. Even while we were running from those bastards."

"Yep."

"That'll get you an A plus too."

It wasn't just a quick escape he'd plotted as windows shattered and gunfire cracked the air all around them, but a rescue plan as well. She found that as sexy as his smile, as sexy as what he'd done to her with his fingers and his focus and his sensitivity to her bliss. Blame four years of being with a man whose solutions to the problems he kept bringing down on their house were anything but. Just snappy answers he'd pulled from his ass at the eleventh hour.

She didn't need a man to take care of her, but it sure was nice when one was up to the task.

"You start to feel drowsy, you let me know, okay?" she said.

"Is that your way of telling me you're feeling drowsy?"

"Kinda. Yeah."

"All right, well. Don't you worry. I'll wake you up if I need to."

"Good."

"But I won't need to."

"All right, well…"

The next thing she knew she was coming up out of a dead sleep as something slammed against the cabin's door with enough force to bring the entire structure down.

She was standing before she knew what was happening.

The fire in the stove still burned. But the stack of wood in the corner was shorter by a third. And there was a new, soft light all around her. Daylight, she realized. Or the earliest, faintest version of peeking in around the edges of the boarded up window and through little cracks in the walls it had been too dark to see the night before.

My God, how long had she slept?

Gun raised, Danny was advancing on the door.

"State your name!" he bellowed.

A voice on the other side. "The fucking sheriff of fucking Surrender, Montana. How's that, you crazy dipshit?"

Danny took a deep breath. His entire frame sagged.

He holstered his gun, undid the padlock, and threw open the door. There stood Cooper MacKenzie, in uniform, with the same dazzling eyes that were practically the man's signature.

Cooper said, "I'm going to go out on a limb here and say you might know something about these two dead jackasses out here in the woods."

6

"I want to see them," Eliza said.

"Trust me," Danny answered. "You don't."

He'd just returned to the cabin after taking to the woods with Coop and the three locals he'd deputized for the very simple reason they all owned Ford pickups capable of making the drive there. An access road led to the Flynns' hunting cabin, but it was as iced over as the rest of the town, which meant even once the snow had died down, a twenty-minute drive had taken their search party almost three hours.

Danny had seen some bad accidents since he'd joined the force. But the bloody scene Cooper had led them to halfway down the hill was one for the books, that was for sure.

"Danny—"

"I know. I know, Eliza. I get it. They tried to kill us so you need to be sure they're dead. So trust me. They are. They are very, very dead."

"What happened?"

"The Explorer got stuck about halfway down the slope. Looks like one of them got out to push and then he got stuck in the snow. So the other one got out to help get him get the Explorer unstuck. And that's when the Explorer decided to get unstuck at just the wrong moment and it went sliding backward down the hill and now... Funny thing is the Explorer made it out okay but that's because their heads cushioned most of the, you know…"

"Oh, wow," she whispered, going pale.

Her hands shook around the plastic coffee cup one of the guys had given her. She no longer had the stomach for the steaming brew, that was clear.

"How stupid were these guys?" she asked, once she had control of herself. "What, were they meth cooks or something?"

"Explorer's a rental, apparently. So they weren't from around here. And IDing them isn't going to be the easiest, given they don't have heads anymore. They've got IDs on them but they're probably fake. We'll run them anyway. See what turns up."

Cooper stepped inside the cabin and closed the door behind him with a loud *thunk* intended to get their attention.

"Eliza," he said. "What do you say we get you back to the station?"

"Sure. That sounds fine. Danny?"

"I need a moment with Danny, actually," Coop said. "You go on ahead with Fred and Bill. They're waiting outside."

Leave now, without Danny? her expression seemed to say.

He gave her a nod and a smile; he tried to keep the latter professional, but apparently it held a trace of what he'd done to her the night before because as soon as Eliza had stepped past him and through the door, Coop cleared his throat and raised an eyebrow.

Once they were alone, the sheriff said, "I oughta ring your neck for taking off your radio."

"Funny. She said the same thing."

"Or fire you. I could always fire you."

"That too. 'Course if you do that first then you don't have cause to ring my neck."

"Says who?"

"The law."

"Oh, good. So we're gonna give the *law* precedence now?

That's rich, Patterson. That's real rich."

"She'd be dead if it wasn't for me, Sheriff."

"I'm aware of that. And for a while there, I thought you were both dead, which is why I'm in a better mood right now than I should be."

"I'm not sure I'm following."

"We found your patrol car around midnight last night but we couldn't see three feet in this storm and there was no driving in it. That said, I had Greyson stay up at the Laughlin Place just in case any of you came back. But that was the best we could do until the storm weakened."

"Thank you. I appreciate that, Sheriff."

"Well, it wasn't my favorite thing, knowing one of my men was out here and not being able to do a damn thing about it. And if you'd turned tail and come back to the station when I'd said, it wouldn't have happened. But then…"

"Eliza would be dead."

"Pretty much. And the whole thing gave me some time to work the phones, get in touch with her ex-husband. That's when things got interesting."

"Did you reach him?"

"No, I reached the FBI agents who stopped him from boarding a flight to Australia last night at LAX. If his inbound plane hadn't been diverted because of the same front that's kicking the shit out of most of the plains states, they probably would have lost him."

"Wait a minute. So he's not being held hostage?"

"By the FBI, yes. And I believe they call it *in custody*. Tell me. What does Eliza know about her ex-husband's business dealings?"

"She thinks he got involved in stolen cars. Something about guys who'd use visas that were about to expire to buy luxury cars and then drop them on a ship for Asia where they'd resell them."

"Well, that's one way of putting it. Lance Laughlin, it turns out, was keeping paperwork and holding stolen cars for one of the largest Russian mafia-run car theft rings in the country. In *history*, maybe. In fact, these guys were running so many stolen cars through the Port of Los Angeles, Lance figured they wouldn't miss a couple Porsche Panameras."

"Lance gets threatened by the Russian mob so he sends Eliza out here to get some cash for them and then he tries to hop a plane? I'm not following."

"Because the story starts much earlier. The Feds took down the major players in this ring a few weeks ago and ever since then the underlings have been fighting over the scraps. What our friends with the Bureau think is that our dead guys out there were two errand boys who knew what Lance was up to and came asking for a cut of the cars he stole once the big fish were out of the pond."

"So why send Eliza out here to get the money?'

"How much did she know about what Lance was up to?"

"She said she asked some questions, but when he got evasive, she didn't push. Divorce was almost final by then. What does that have to..."

And then it hit him like a ton of bricks.

"I know," Coop said when he saw the expression on Danny's face. "Give yourself a minute to take it all in. It's a big one."

"He sent her out here to get killed. 'Cause she asked a few questions."

"Something like that, yeah."

"Walk me through it if you can, Sheriff. It's been a long night."

"Okay. So Tweedle Shithead and Tweedle Headless down there come knocking on Lance's door, asking for a cut of the *stolen* stolen cars. Lance tells them the money's buried on his family's property in Surrender. And those idiots are dumb enough to believe him. So while they're booking tickets to Kalispell, Lance thinks, *Damn. Lucky break! I better flee the country before more of this mess shows up on my front step.* But first, there's the small matter of his ex-wife, who asked a few too many questions. So he picks up the phone and sends her out here to have a run-in with two of the stupidest and greediest assholes in the history of West Coast organized crime."

"'Cause if they run into each other when she's got a shovel on her, the guys will assume Eliza stole the money no matter what she says."

"If there even *is* any money buried on that property."

"So he sent her out here to die," Danny growled. "That fucking son of a bitch literally sent her out here to get killed."

"That's what it looks like... Hey, Danny..."

But it was too late. He'd kicked the stack of firewood and sent half of it rolling across the cabin floor like bowling balls. Cooper held up his hands and bowed his head, as if Danny's fury had taken the form of a cloud that needed time to fill the cabin briefly before it vaporized.

"You good?" Coop finally asked.

"One sec."

He picked up one of the pieces of firewood he'd knocked over and threw it at the opposing wall so hard it cracked into two pieces before it hit the floor.

"Now I'm better," he said, but he sounded like a fire-breathing dragon trying to master English. "I don't suppose Lance actually confessed to all of this."

"He did. To his new girlfriend. The one who was going to flee the country with him. The same one who made the mistake of selling topless photos of her high school friends to some guys on the Internet who were not in high school."

"So the girlfriend's singing to avoid child porn charges?"

"Pretty much, yeah."

They just stood there for a while.

"You're a good deputy, Danny. But I've kept you clear of the kind of work my cousins do, 'cause this is what it's like. Brushes with pure evil. That kind of thing, it'll change you, for sure. You can't control that. But you can control how it changes you. So try looking on the bright side. That's my recommendation. Yes, Lance Laughlin turned out to be a murderous bastard with no conscience, but he also got hit with some of the worst luck of any criminal on the planet. And that's proof of a hopeful universe, if you ask me."

"I understand, Sheriff."

"And you and Eliza are still alive. That's the most important thing."

"Thank you, sir."

"FBI's got agents on their way here soon as the storm clears out for good and the airstrip in Myrna Springs opens again. In the meantime, they've asked us to start digging on the Laughlin ranch to see if this money even exists. You're coming back to the station with me. FBI wants to put Eliza on the phone and have a conversation with her. Only good side of that is that they'll have to break this news to her instead of us."

"So I can't tell her anything?"

"Not yet, no. But you can be there when she finds out."

"I understand, Sheriff."

"One thing's for sure. Lance Laughlin is one of the baddest apples Surrender's ever produced."

"I don't supposed we can blame him on Los Angeles."

"To be honest, I don't suppose we can blame him on any place in particular, much as I'd like to."

It seemed like they were finished, but Cooper stayed in the door, giving Danny a long, cool once-over.

"Long night here in this cabin," he said. "What did y'all get up to?"

"You mean aside from staying alive?"

"Yes. Aside from staying alive."

Danny couldn't meet the sheriff's gaze.

"All right," Cooper said. "Well, congratulations, kid. But know this. You may think you were big guns last night. But the time to show her what a man you are is now, soon as this news washes over her like a tidal wave. And trust me. Keeping her from drowning in it isn't going to be easy and it's going to take every ounce of grown-up you got."

7

Even over the phone the Feds were bossy as hell.

They'd asked everyone to leave the room, except for Eliza and Cooper, which had left Danny hovering outside. The room in question was Coop's personal office, thanks to a town council that had twice blocked funding for the type of interrogation rooms you saw on T.V. shows.

He figured he should count his blessings.

Being forced to stand outside a closed, solid door while dispatch fielded calls about downed power lines and escaped livestock probably wasn't so bad, all things considered. Watching Eliza's emotional destruction through a one-way mirror without being able to take her in his arms might have been a form of torture on par with waterboarding.

So he put his best game face on and ignored the curious looks the dispatcher kept giving him in between calls. Hopefully Deputy Greyson would be back soon. Greyson wouldn't give him any shit about what he'd done, that was for sure. Just a few feet from Danny was the jail cell where Greyson had gotten down and dirty with an old flame he'd taken into custody, an old flame to whom he was now married.

Still, being separated from Eliza filled Danny with fear. Like Lance Laughlin's dark energy might somehow reach through the sheriff's phone and spirit her away for good.

When the door popped open and Coop stepped out, every muscle in Danny's body tensed. He locked eyes with his boss and mentor, heard again the challenge the man had issued him before they'd left the hunting cabin.

"You're up," Coop finally said.

Now's the time to prove you're all grown up, he thought.

He stepped past Coop and into the tiny office.

The last time he'd seen a woman this wrecked was the day after his father had walked out on them for good and he'd come across his mother, sitting by herself in the living room, staring past the wedding photo she was holding loosely in both hands.

Eliza sat on the edge of her chair, arms resting on the front of Coop's desk, staring vacantly at the opposite wall. There were no tears in her eyes. This frightened Danny even more. Tears he knew how to handle. Scoop her up. Take her in his arms, whisper assurances into her sweet-smelling hair. That was how you dealt with tears.

This was something altogether different. A blend of anger and darkness that threatened to take Eliza away from him, away from *everyone*, for a very long time.

"Did you know?" she asked.

"Coop told me back at the cabin. But the Feds wanted us to stay quiet until they talked to you."

"I understand," she whispered.

Danny took a seat. It didn't help. Settling into the sheriff's chair made him feel like he was just playacting at this whole grown up thing.

He reached across the desk and placed a hand over hers. She closed her eyes. But he couldn't tell if she was savoring his touch.

He hoped so.

God, he hoped so.

"Listen, I know I talk too damn much, but I need to tell you a story. It's partly a story about why I talk so damn much, but I wouldn't be telling it if I didn't think it would help." *Don't tell her how to feel,* he thought. *Not right now.* "If I didn't *want* it to help, I mean."

Eliza nodded, but she was staring at the empty desk. She adjusted her hand just enough so that she hooked one of his fingers in between her own.

"I'm the reason my father left when I was fourteen," he said. "Well, not really. I mean, I'm not the reason he was driving truckloads of drugs over the Canadian border for the del Fuego cartel. But I'm the reason my mother found out about it, and I'm the reason he ran. See, he had two cell phones. One for us and his job with Rawley Beamis. The other was for the del Fuegos. And one day, I saw the second phone and I said something to my mom about it. That was all.

"I had no idea what he was up to. I just thought it was strange that he had two phones, is all. And I thought it was something Mom should know. Like maybe there was another woman or something. Anyway, once I asked the question, Mom turned around and started asking him questions and that's when he ran. That's when he picked drug money over us."

He had her full attention now.

"So for a week I blamed myself. I was the reason he ran. If I'd just kept my big mouth shut, he'd still be at home. He'd still be her husband and he'd still be my dad. I mean, people had always told me I talked too much so it made perfect sense, didn't it? Danny's big mouth blows it yet again. So I just stopped talking altogether. I held my momma while she cried but I barely said anything cause it was me saying too much that had caused all this pain in the first place."

Eliza shook her head to protest.

Danny held up his free hand to stop her.

"Finally, Momma backed me to the wall and asked me why I was being so quiet. And I just exploded. I broke down into tears and told her everything I was feeling. How I thought I was responsible for it all. I told her I was never going to speak again. That I'd speak only when spoken to. That I'd stop asking so many questions and having opinions about stuff. I swore it up and down the living room while she listened to me cry. I must've swore it a dozen times.

"Then, once I'd managed to calm myself, she told me something I'll never forget. She said my father was a bad man and bad men use your goodness against you. They take what you do to help others and they use it for their own bad ends, and when they walk away, leaving you destroyed inside, they count on you feeling like your goodness was to blame. Like your goodness was just a weakness and you should have known better. What destroyed my family was that my father decided to run drugs for the del Fuego cartel. And when we found out the truth, he chose them over us. Period. End of story.

"And I don't know if you've noticed, but I never kept my pledge. I never stopped asking all sorts of questions and I never stopped having opinions and I never stopped trying to talk my way to the truth of the matter. Because my mother told me I couldn't. Because my mother told me I wasn't allowed to let my father break me like that. To let his *crimes* break me like that."

The story had earned him her full attention. But there wasn't pity in her eyes, thank God. Instead, she was regarding him as an equal, as someone who shared in her pain without lecturing her about it or dismissing it or trying to call it something other than what it was—pain. And only now did he realize she'd taken his hand in hers while he'd talked. Now her grip was firm.

"Good," she whispered.

"Yes, that's good, and what'll also be good is if you don't allow yourself to think for one moment that you were almost killed last night because you were too trusting or too helpful, or just too determined not to see anyone get killed, even if that person was your ex-husband. What happened last night to you, to *us*, happened because Lance Laughlin is a criminal and he was determined to do whatever he could to cover his tracks and leave the country. It didn't happen because you're weak. It didn't happen because you cared too much. It didn't happen because you opened your heart and loved him once."

Now the tears slipped easily from her eyes. She closed her hand around his and gripped it firmly.

"Truth is I've only been on the job a year, Eliza. I've never fought in the military, and the most violent offenders I've dealt with up close are drunk and disorderlies and pissed-off horses. So I don't have some big wise speech to give you about the evils I've seen with my own two eyes. I only have my own story, my own past. So just know that if I'd kept my pledge to my mother that night, if I'd stopped asking questions and barging my way into things with my mouth in the lead, I never would have gone up there last night, and if I hadn't gone up there then..."

"I'd be dead," she whispered.

Three simple words, but they unleashed the full force of her pain and sadness. He rose, pulled the empty chair in front of the desk up close to hers and took her in his arms. The fight went out of her body. She wilted against him as the sobs shook her.

"But you're not," he said after a while. "You're not dead."

At these words, she held him tighter, as if the feel of him was the best confirmation of this fact.

8

"Where you headed, mister?" Eliza asked.

Danny had just tucked her into his bed, but now he seemed eager to leave her alone. One hand on the bedroom door, he turned and looked at her through the flickering shadows. While she'd showered, he'd lit some scented candles throughout his tiny house—maybe pumpkin spice, but she wasn't sure—and drawn the window shade.

His place was tiny and he'd been too busy during the run-up to the storm to haul the pieces of his outdoor gym inside, so when the two of them had walked through the backyard, they'd found his free weights and benches iced over like something out of a horror movie about the end of the world. Inside, however, the one-bedroom house was spotless and quaint, in that way that straight men try to make things quaint. By hiding their mess in drawers and hanging small family photos in random spots along the walls.

Now, after a shower and changing into some boxers and a T-shirt he'd given her, she was snuggled into the warmest and most comfortable bed she'd ever experienced. But she wasn't sure what made it feel that way—the awful night she'd had, or that it was Danny's bed.

"Thought I'd shower," he said. "Give you some time to rest."

"I slept most of the night. You're the one who needs some rest."

"Still. I wasn't sure if..."

"Wasn't sure if what?" she asked.

He bowed his head, blinked, trying to find his words, a series of moves that made him seem both innocent and chivalrous.

"I don't want to sleep alone, if that's what you're asking."

"Okay," he answered. "Okay. Sure."

"But I do want to sleep. I mean, I probably need to sleep some more. You *certainly* need to sleep, that's for sure."

"Sure. Right."

"Take a shower, Danny. Then come get in bed with me."

"Sure," he answered, only this time the word didn't come out sounding robotic.

Soon FBI agents would arrive in Surrender with more questions. Soon she'd have to dig up the entire sad story of her marriage for a room full of impassive government men. Or at least she thought they'd be all men and she thought they'd look impassive because that's how it always was in the movies, and right now movies were the only frame of reference she had for a situation this insane.

But those were worries for tomorrow or the next day. In the meantime, the agents had made it clear that Lance was going down, and they had his new girlfriend to thank for that.

Today was about Danny's bed, and Danny. Today was about imagining what Danny looked like in the shower as water sluiced down his hard, young body.

Maybe she should join him. Had he refrained from joining her under the spray moments before because he thought she wasn't ready to be touched?

She did want to be touched.

Hard.

Shameful! Just shameful to be thinking such lustful thoughts in this moment. She should be devastated, destroyed. Tearing the room apart in a rage. She'd almost died, after all. Worse, she'd almost been murdered.

Emphasis on *almost*, thanks to the gorgeous young man showering a few feet away.

Was she obligated to be upset? Was she obligated to ignore her attraction to Danny for at least another twenty-four hours? If so, that just seemed like another win for her bastard ex. And if the answer to those questions was no, that left her with another dilemma.

Was she using her desire for Danny as a distraction and nothing more?

He probably wouldn't mind if that was the case. But she would.

The more she thought about it, the more the answer to her question seemed implicit in the phrasing she'd just used.

Desire.

Being an English teacher for years had taught her one incontrovertible fact.

No matter what the dictionary said, everyone had their own personal definitions of the words they used. And for her, desire was more than lust; it was more than hunger or passing fancy. Desire was what you felt for the man under the muscles when he did something more than ask you to follow him on Instagram.

Desire was what you felt when a man used his muscles to save your life.

Desire was what she felt for Danny Patterson right now as he stepped into the bedroom, a towel wrapped around his waist, the hard ridges of his torso glistening with droplets of water.

Yes, it was a young body—a young, hard body that would have made most of her girlfriends squeal—but most men twice his age weren't capable of doing the things he'd done for her these past twenty-four hours. Not because those things required stamina or physical strength. They'd required courage, a level of courage that had nothing to do with age and everything to do with character. And if he'd just been some smooth, skinned hulk of muscle, she would have felt nothing for him in this moment. But the things he'd done for her, the risks he'd taken, the sacrifices he'd made, those things had stepped out of the shower with him and now electrified the air in the darkened, candle-lit bedroom.

"Just need to get some clothes," he said quietly.

"No, you don't."

He went still, straightening.

"I wasn't sure you..."

"Wasn't sure I'd what? Be in the mood?"

"Something like that, yeah."

"After you saved my life? Lord, what do women usually make you do to win their affection? Wrestle grizzly bears in a pit of vipers?"

"I hate snakes."

"Me too."

He started toward the bed, still holding the towel at one corner of his waist, steps slow and careful.

"And I wouldn't know anything about other women," he said.

"Don't tell me you're a virgin."

She wasn't sure if the idea frightened her or thrilled her. She'd never taken a man's virginity before, unless, of course, you counted the man who'd taken her own, a nervous high school boyfriend. And it hadn't felt like either of them was *taking* much of anything, per se. More like they'd just sort of bumped into each other in the dark and ended up sweaty and confused. Kind of like stumbling into someone in a haunted house only to discover they were another frightened visitor and not one of the actors dressed as psychotic clowns.

"So if I was, you wouldn't want me to tell you?" he asked. He took a seat on the edge of the bed, just within her reach.

"I didn't say that."

"You said not to tell you if I was a virgin," he reminded her.

"You're not a virgin."

"How would you know?"

"Because you look like that. Girls are probably throwing themselves at you all the time. And here I am, looking like I should drive carpool."

"Some of the best women in the world drive carpool, Eliza."

"True, but it doesn't exactly burn calories."

"Yeah, well, I've got a good plan for that, Miss Brightwell."

"You're just saying anything to get me in bed. Which is kinda silly considering I'm already in your bed and I want you to get in here with me."

"Yeah, but you've still got clothes on," he said with a grin.

"You gave me these clothes."

"Huge mistake."

"Doesn't mean you can't take 'em off."

"You sure you don't want to rest?" he asked.

"No, I'd much rather use every inch of your body to avoid dealing with post traumatic stress or whatever it is I'm probably about to be diagnosed with."

"I'm not sure how I feel about being objectified," he said with a huge grin that said he loved the idea.

"Well, you're not feeling anything yet. You need to get in bed for that part."

"Still, I'm nervous..."

"About what?"

"I just...I want this to be just right," he said. "You're not some girl in a bar. You're Eliza Brightwell and I want to do everything to make this perfect."

"Tell me you're not serious," she said.

"Of course I'm serious," he said, the hurt evident in his voice.

"No, Danny. That's not it. It's... You saved my life. You

kept me alive during a blizzard with just some wood and a stove."

"And a Buick. Don't forget the Buick."

"I haven't. I won't. My point is, what else could you possibly do to make this perfect?"

"You really mean that?"

"I can't lie to you, Danny. Not after last night. And not after what you told me back at the station. I could never lie to you again."

Only once the words were out of her mouth did she realize they sounded like some kind of vow. Because they were here. A promise. A promise that wasn't about the next forty-five minutes they spent together in his bed, or the next few weeks she was probably going to be forced to spend in Surrender. The promise she'd just made to Danny was about the future, a future she wanted him to be a part of.

"Never lie to me again?" he asked with a broad grin. "That makes it sound like we're going to be spending a lot of time together. Are we?"

"Can we? Please?"

"You don't have to say please, Eliza. Not this time."

"Okay... Then get in bed with me."

"All right, well, just as long as you're sure you're not doing this because you think you owe me."

"What?" She pulled the towel free of his grip with one tug. It slid down his hard thighs then slipped over his knees before falling to the carpet, revealing his cock at the ready. "This?"

He looked powerful and strong, but also exposed and vulnerable, and the combination shortened her breaths, made her face flush. There was something about the innocent, expectant expression and his thick, gasp-inducing erection that nailed her to the mattress, made her pulse ring in her ears. Unlike many of her girlfriends, she didn't want a man to take relentless control, to bend her over the hood of his car and ask questions later. She wanted a man who tested, tasted, and adjusted based on her response. She wanted a man who could take instructions. She'd never tied a man up, but she liked to give an order now and then.

This fact of her desire had always shamed her, as if her need to turn a man into a student of her pleasure was a perversion of the years she'd spent as a teacher. Only now did she realize it was Lance who'd put this thought in her head. Whenever she'd tried to guide or instruct him in the bedroom, he'd snarled some version of, "I'm not one of your damn students." In the process, she'd been left with the crazy notion that being honest about her needs somehow put her in league with child molesters.

Time to put that crazy line of thought in jail along with her ex-husband.

Now, Danny Patterson filled those hidden and overlooked parts of herself with lust and light, and she had no choice but to explore them.

In his bed, with his hand reaching up to draw the comforter off her body. With his hard, muscular body glistening in the light from the bathroom, his cock engorged and jerking just from the anticipation of touching her.

It was, without a doubt, the most erotic thing she'd ever felt, the feel of his hard, naked body coming to rest atop hers, and its deliciousness was compounded by the fact that he didn't rush to pull her clothes off. He kissed her instead. Taking all the sweet time they didn't have up in that tiny hunting cabin. Her hands roamed his back, gripping the tight cheeks of his ass, savoring the hard flesh of him as their tongues found their perfect, intimate rhythm.

Then, after a while—she had no idea how long, exactly—her breaths were so rapid and high pitched he took them as a sign they'd passed a point of no return. He reared up onto his haunches, slid his old T-shirt up and over her breasts.

At the sight of her body exposed, he let out a small, controlled growl, the sound of a good and patient boy deciding to turn bad.

He kneaded, pinched, teased and nibbled, searching for spots that made her back arch and her toes curl. Once he slid his boxers down her legs, he leaned in close to her aching, moistened folds and inhaled. No man had ever done this to her before, taken in the raw scent of her as if it were deliciously hypnotic.

In the past, it was moments like these when she'd forced herself to stay silent, even as the desire to direct welled within her. This wasn't the past. This was now. This was new. Not Lance, but Danny. Gorgeous, devoted and brave.

"Now, Danny," she said. "Now…make me…"

"Now what?" he asked, his lips so close to her pussy his breath tickled her folds.

"Do it."

"Do what, Eliza?" He placed his ring and index fingers on either side of her bud, grazing the edges of it, then closing his fingers so that on the return trip, he gave it a long, determined swipe.

"Fuck me, Danny."

"Now? You mean, you want me to skip…"

He gave her a clit a gentle lick.

"No," she gasped. "I want you to fuck me with your tongue, you sweet, dirty boy."

That was all he needed. He started with a mad, focused flicker. Soon her bones felt molten and her thighs were rising off the bed, gripping his neck. He slid his hands under her ass and gripped her cheeks, drawing her sex harder against his hungry, working mouth. She was cursing. Screaming. Thanking God he didn't have neighbors even as she thanked God for his gifted tongue.

"Am I doing a good job?" he asked, breathless. "Am I doing a good job of eating your pussy, Miss Brightwell?"

Oh, that was so like him, to spring the role-play on her now when it felt delicious and dirty and absolutely perfect.

"You're doing a great job, Danny," she gasped. "Now sit

up and let me see what a man you've grown up to be."

He rocked back onto his haunches, his weight rolling off her, freeing her to rear up and crawl toward his cock—his beautiful, statuesque cock, which she took tenderly in both hands before sliding them gently along its length, a simple, light gesture that caused him to shudder. He let out a long, stuttering moan.

Was he about to come?

She released him just in case.

He drew several deep breaths to steady himself, then reached down and twined his fingers gently through her hair. She took that as a sign to go back to work.

"Eliza…"

"Yes, Danny."

He didn't shudder or groan as she stroked him, but he did bite his lower lip.

"Eliza…"

It was like her name had become a mantra designed to keep him connected to his body even as her touch alone threatened to blast him into the heavens.

"Yes, Danny," she said, and gave the head of his cock a swift, gentle lick.

"Eliza. You are…"

"Yes?"

"You are…"

Before he could answer, she licked the length of his cock, squeezing the head in her palm. Then she gripped his shaft, swallowed his head and established two contrasting rhythms.

"Eliza…"

She groaned and kept working.

"Eliza!"

He went from gently stroking her head to gripping it.

"*Eliza!*"

She recognized a note of alarm in his voice, put two and

two together, and got her mouth off his cock just in time.

He fell back onto his haunches, cock jerking as he erupted. God, it was a sight, and the beauty of it chased away her disappointment over having brought them here too quickly. The silent O of his mouth, the rippling tension shooting through his every visible muscle, the ropes of cum flying from his cock. It was like a Baroque sculpture carved by a filthy pervert.

Just at the moment when she thought he'd start apologizing and her own gratification would be delayed, Danny jumped off the side of the bed.

"Just one minute!"

"Wait…what? Where are you going?"

It all happened so fast. He was back on the bed and on top of her in no time. She'd heard the faucet run for a few seconds, and she'd glimpsed him tossing a hand towel behind him as he emerged from the bathroom. Then their mouths were inches apart and she was realizing he was clean and not remotely sticky as he kissed her and smoothed her hair back from her forehead.

"Five minutes," he said with a smile.

"I'm sorry. What?"

"Just give me five minutes and I'll be ready to go again."

"Danny, you don't have to…"

"Yes, I do. I do have to. And I want to."

"Danny, you've been up all night. Let's just get some rest and then maybe we can—"

"Five minutes," he said with a smile.

"Danny. I wasn't born yesterday, okay? I know it's gonna take a lot longer than five minutes."

His mouth to her, he growled, "Trust me. It won't. There are advantages to being with a younger man, Miss Brightwell."

"Okay. Okay. Let's not put it exactly like that. That makes it sound a little—"

"How about I put it like this?" He took her right nipple

gently between his teeth while he rolled the left between his thumb and finger. Suckling. Nibbling. Pinching. Kneading. Working his way back down her body. Returning to places he'd visited just moments before, only this time gently, leisurely, but persistently. Bringing her back to the place of burning hunger and aching need she'd been in when she'd reared up and taken his cock in both hands.

He surfaced after a while, kissing her as he rubbed his fresh erection against her folds, showing her how much he could feel for her and how quickly.

Advantages indeed, she thought.

"Give me permission," he growled into her ear.

"Permission to what?" she teased.

"To fuck you so hard you can't remember where you are. To fuck you so hard the only thing you know is that it's me on top of you. Me inside you. Me tasting you. Me making you come so hard you feel like you're gonna fly apart and I'm the only thing that can hold you together."

"Yes," she whispered.

"Yes, what, Eliza?"

"Fuck me, Danny. Fuck me like you've always wanted to."

She'd lost herself in his dirty talk; the sound of the nightstand drawer sliding open and the brief ritual of the condom were vague suggestions. She couldn't remember the last time she'd been this ready, this open. Maybe there hadn't been a last time. Because it had never been him. It had never been Danny. Danny, who could read her body and her mind. Danny, who shared not only this electric intimacy, but who, during one of her lowest moments, had shared a story straight from his heart, a story designed to comfort and protect. And now he had sealed their bodies together, driving into her as he suckled her neck.

She'd never had a man take her quite like this, a man who managed to bury himself inside her without losing eye contact. A man who could kiss while he fucked. Two separate rhythms, sometimes meeting and overlapping, sometimes contrasting. Together they made for a sense of absolute connection.

This time, the bliss was a slow build, a heat that spread from her sex to the rest of her body. Pulsing in waves that forced her to close her eyes. Each pulse was so intense she couldn't look at him and breathe at the same time. She had to choose between one or the other, and it didn't matter, because even when she closed her eyes there was still Danny and only Danny. Driving, kissing, grunting, saying her name like the very sound of it sustained him. And when the pulses turned into a single wash of pleasure that shot through her from head to toe, he increased his thrusts. Didn't vary the rhythm. Drove hard but steady, his every muscle now devoted to her gratification and release. And when she finally came, it felt like a hard shell inside of her cracked, and the terror and regret of the past few days came tumbling out before he drove them away with a series of powerful thrusts.

"Hey," he whispered.

And that's when she realized she was crying. He settled down next to her, reached down and slid the condom off so it wouldn't irritate her as he snuggled up to her.

She tried to speak, but she couldn't. She didn't regret what they'd done, not for a second. But she'd never experienced this kind of emotional release before coming so quickly on the back of pure pleasure. If there was such a thing as therapeutic orgasm—and Lord knows, someone in California had probably already come up with the term—this was it. Right here.

"Hey," he whispered gently.

"So good," she managed through her tears. "No...so good..."

"Okay," he whispered, stroking the side of her cheek with one bent finger. "Okay."

"Just. So much, you know? So much but...so good."

She'd heard about this from friends who'd been to

chiropractors, that some muscle would get released in the course of their session and all sorts of emotions would come tumbling out. This was a version of that, times ten.

After a few minutes, he gently whisked her lingering tears away with a finger, which tickled her cheeks and caused her to giggle.

"I guess after what we've been through there was a lot of pent-up energy there," he said.

"There was a lot of pent-up everything."

"But it's out now."

"Yeah, I guess."

"You don't sound happy."

"No...no. It's just... All the frustration and all the anger, you can't get rid of it all at once, I don't think. It's always going to be around. But with you here, it's..."

"So you want to go again?" he asked. "See if we can get the rest of it?"

Was he kidding? When she saw his big, mischievous grin, she cracked up. A second, less intense release.

"Oh, Danny."

"Oh, Eliza."

"I don't ever want to leave this bed," she said before she could think twice about it.

"Who said you had to?"

"Eventually..."

"Eventually what?"

"You're sure you're not going to get sick of me once the whole drama fades? Once you realize everything I put you through?"

"There you go again. Blaming yourself for things you didn't do."

"Give me time."

"I will," he said. "I will give you time. Lots of time, Eliza. Time for this to become exactly what it needs to be. Time for you to stay in this bed, my bed, for as long as you want."

She wanted to protest. She wanted to call him a silly boy. Wanted to dismiss him, contain him. Because sometimes it was easier to go back to old habits and bad situations than it was to embrace the future, especially when the future was as beautiful and bright and exceptional as Danny Patterson. Deputy Danny Patterson, proud member of the Surrender Sheriff's Department, who had saved her from bullets and ice and two crazy criminals who didn't know shit about snow and cars.

"Are you sure, Danny?"

"Yes, I'm sure."

"Good. 'Cause I'm going to need a lot of time in this bed, and a lot of time with you."

Another unhurried kiss, another close embrace.

"With me, Eliza, you've got all the time you need and we can spend it wherever you like."

Sign up for the 1001 Dark Nights Newsletter
and be entered to win a Tiffany Lock necklace.

There's a contest every quarter!

Go to www.1001DarkNights.com to subscribe.

Discover the Liliana Hart MacKenzie Family Collection

Trouble Maker
A MacKenzie Family Novel
by Liliana Hart

Marnie Whitlock has never known what it's like to be normal. She and her family moved from place to place, hiding from reporters and psychologists, all because of her gift. A curse was more like it. Seeing a victim, feeling his pain as the last of his life ebbed away, and being helpless to save him. It was torture. And then one day it disappeared and she was free. Until those who hunted her for her gift tried to kill her. And then the gift came back with a vengeance.

Beckett Hamilton leads a simple life. His ranch is profitable and a legacy he'll be proud to pass onto his children one day, work fills his time from sunup to sundown, and his romances are short and sweet. He wouldn't have it any other way. And then he runs into quiet and reserved Marnie Whitlock just after she moves to town. She intrigues him like no woman ever has. And she's hiding something. His hope is that she begins to trust him before it's too late.

* * * *

Rush
A MacKenzie Family Novella
by Robin Covington

From Liliana Hart's New York Times bestselling MacKenzie family comes a new story by USA Today bestselling author Robin Covington...

Atticus Rush doesn't really like people. Years in Special Ops and law enforcement showed him the worst of humanity, making his mountain hideaway the ideal place to live. But when his colleagues at MacKenzie Security need him to save the kidnapped young daughter of a U.S. Senator, he'll do it, even if it means working with the woman who broke his heart ...his ex-wife.

Lady Olivia Rutledge-Cairn likes to steal things. Raised with a silver spoon and the glass slipper she spent years cultivating a cadre of acquaintances in the highest places. She parlayed her natural gift for theft into a career of locating and illegally retrieving hard-to-find items of value for the ridiculously wealthy. Rush was the one man who tempted her to change her ways...until he caught her and threatened to turn her in.

MacKenzie Security has vowed to save the girl. Olivia can find anything or anyone. Rush can get anyone out. As the clock winds down on the girl's life, can they fight the past, a ruthless madman and their explosive passion to get the job done?

* * * *

Bullet Proof
A MacKenzie Family Novella
by Avery Flynn

"Being one of the good guys is not my thing."

Bianca Sutherland isn't at an exclusive Eyes-Wide-Shut style orgy for the orgasms. She's there because the only clue to her friend's disappearance is a photo of a painting hanging somewhere in Bisu Manor. Determined to find her missing friend when no one else will, she expects trouble when she cons her way into the party—but not in the form of a so-hot-he-turns-your-panties-to-ash former boxer.

Taz Hazard's only concern is looking out for himself and he has no intention of changing his ways until he finds sexy-as-sin Bianca at the most notorious mansion in Ft. Worth. Now, he's tangled up in a missing person case tied into a powerful new drug about to flood the streets, if they can't find a way to stop it before its too late. Taking on a drug cartel isn't safe, but when passion ignites between them Taz and Bianca discover their hearts aren't bulletproof either.

* * * *

Delta: Rescue
A MacKenzie Family Novella
by Cristin Harber

When Luke Brenner takes an off-the-books job on the MacKenzie-Delta joint task force, he has one goal: shut down sex traffickers on his personal hunt for retribution. This operation brings him closer than he's ever been to avenge his first love, who was taken, sold, and likely dead.

Madeleine Mercier is the daughter of an infamous cartel conglomerate. Their family bleeds money, they sell pleasure, they sell people. She knows no other life, sees no escape, except for one. Maddy is the only person who can take down Papa, when every branch of law enforcement in every country, is on her father's payroll.

It's evil. To want to ruin, to murder, her family. But that's what she is. Ruined for a life outside of destroying her father. She can't feel arousal. Has never been kissed. Never felt anything other than disgust for the world that she perpetuates. Until she clashes with a possible mercenary who gives her hope.

The hunter versus the virgin. The predator and his prey. When forced together, can enemies resist the urge to run away or destroy one another?

* * * *

Deep Trouble
A MacKenzie Family Novella
by Kimberly Kincaid

Bartender Kylie Walker went into the basement of The Corner Tavern for a box of cocktail napkins, but what she got was an eyeful of murder. Now she's on the run from a killer with connections, and one wrong step could be her last. Desperate to stay safe, Kylie calls the only person she trusts—her ex-Army Ranger brother. The only problem? He's two thousand miles away, and trouble is right outside her door.

Security specialist Devon Randolph might be rough and gruff, but he'll never turn down a friend in need, especially when that friend is the fellow Ranger who once saved his life. Devon may have secrets, but he's nearby, and he's got the skills to keep his buddy's sister safe…even if one look at brash, beautiful, Kylie makes him want to break all the rules.

Forced on the run, Kylie and Devon dodge bullets and bad guys, but they cannot fight the attraction burning between them. Yet the closer they grow, the higher the stakes become. Will they be able to outrun a brutal killer? Or will Devon's secrets tear them apart first?

About Christopher Rice

New York Times bestselling author Christopher Rice's first foray into erotic romance, *THE FLAME*, earned accolades from some of the genre's most beloved authors. "Sensual, passionate and intelligent," wrote Lexi Blake, "it's everything an erotic romance should be." J. Kenner called it "absolutely delicious," Cherise Sinclair hailed it as "beautifully lyrical" and Lorelei James announced, "I look forward to reading more!" He went on to publish two more installments in The Desire Exchange Series, *THE SURRENDER GATE* and *KISS THE FLAME*. Prior to his erotic romance debut, Christopher published four *New York Times* bestselling thrillers before the age of 30, received a Lambda Literary Award and was declared one of People Magazine's Sexiest Men Alive. His supernatural thrillers, *THE HEAVENS RISE and THE VINES*, were both nominated for Bram Stoker Awards. Aside from authoring eight works of dark suspense, Christopher is also the co-host and executive producer of THE DINNER PARTY SHOW WITH CHRISTOPHER RICE & ERIC SHAW QUINN, all the episodes of which can be downloaded at www.TheDinnerPartyShow.com and from iTunes. Look for their new You Tube channel in Spring 2016.

Dance of Desire
By Christopher Rice
Coming February 23, 2016

From *New York Times* bestselling author Christopher Rice, comes a steamy, emotional tale of forbidden romance between a woman struggling to get her life on its feet and the gorgeous cowboy her father kept her from marrying years before. The first contemporary romance from Christopher Rice is written with the author's trademark humor and heart, and introduces readers to a beautiful town in the Texas Hill Country called Chapel Springs.

* * * *

"It's a terrible idea," he says.

"Why did she tell you?"

"Because she wants me to stop you."

"That's not true. I talked to her this afternoon and she told me she wanted me to go."

"Well, she must have changed her mind," he says.

"Well, I haven't changed mine."

"A sex club?" he bellows. "What are you? Crazy?"

"Since when are you so full of judgment, cowboy? I've never seen you in church!"

"And I've never seen you in a sex club!"

"Have you been to that many? Who knows? I could have a whole secret life you don't even know about."

"I know who you are, Amber. I know *how* you are."

"And what does that mean?"

"Amber, you stayed a virgin until you were nineteen. That puts you in the, like, one percentile of girls in our high school."

"How do you know that? I never told you that!"

"I had my sources."

"You were keeping tabs on my virginity? That's rich. I thought you were too busy starting fistfights outside the Valley View Mall so you didn't have to feel anything."

"And you were too busy tending to my wounds 'cause it gave you an excuse to look at my chest."

"Get out of my house!"

"Amber—"

"Get out!"

He bows his head. A lesser man would ignore her request, but he knows he's bound by it.

"I shouldn't have said that," Caleb whispers. "I'm sorry."

He turns to leave.

"You know, I forgave you a lot because you lost a lot. But don't you pretend for one second that you joined our family with a smile and a thank you and that was that. Those first few years, it was like living with a tornado. You were *impossible!* An you were nothing like the guy I'd..."

He turns away from the front door. "The guy you'd what?"

"All I'm saying is that even if I'd wanted to…"

"Wanted to what?"

He's closing the distance between them. Her head wants to run from him. Her soul wants to run to him. Her body's forced to split the difference. She's got no choice but to stand there while he advances on her, nostrils flaring, blue eyes blazing.

"Tell me why you really don't want me to go," she hears herself whisper. "Tell me why you—"

He takes her in his arms and rocks them into the wall, so suddenly she expects her head to knock against the wood, but one of his powerful hands cushions the back of her skull just in time.

His lips meet the nape of her neck, grazing, testing. It's hesitant, the kiss he gives her there, as if he's afraid she's an apparition that will vanish if he tries to take a real taste.

He gathers the hem of her shirt into his fist, knuckles grazing the skin of her stomach. She's trying to speak but the only thing coming out of her are stuttering gasps. She's been rendered wordless by the feel of the forbidden, by the weight of the forbidden, by the power of the forbidden.

It's the first time they've touched since that night on the boat dock, if you don't include the light dabs of hydrogen peroxide she'd apply to the wounds he got fighting, usually while they sat together in the kitchen, her parents watching over them nervously. Twelve years living under the same roof and they never shared so much as a hug after that night, nothing that might risk the feel of his skin against her own.

And now this.

Now the intoxicating blend of the cologne he wore as a teenager mingling with the musky aroma of his belt and boots. Now the knowledge that he'd asked after her virginity years before, that the thought of her lying with another man had filled him with protective, jealous rage then just as it does now.

She feels boneless and moist. One of those feelings isn't an illusion.

If this is what it feels like to be bad, she thinks, *no wonder so many people get addicted.*

"Tell me," she whispers. "Tell me why you really don't want me to go."

"I am," he growls.

He presses their foreheads together, takes the sides of her face in both of his large, powerful hands. It's torture, this position. It's deliberate, she's sure. It keeps her from lifting her mouth to his. Keeps her from looking straight into his eyes. He's fighting it, still. Just as she's fought it for years.

She parts her lips, inviting him to kiss her.

"Please," he groans. "Just, please *don't* go."

"Caleb…" She reaches for his face.

On behalf of 1001 Dark Nights,

Liz Berry and M.J. Rose would like to thank ~

Liliana Hart
Scott Silverii
Steve Berry
Doug Scofield
Kim Guidroz
Jillian Stein
InkSlinger PR
Asha Hossain
Kasi Alexander
Chris Graham
Pamela Jamison
Jessica Johns
Dylan Stockton
and Simon Lipskar

CPSIA information can be obtained at www.ICGtesting.com
Printed in the USA
LVOW12s0348150316

479097LV00001B/191/P

9 781942 299332